Holding the Key
To a Hustla's Heart

Leondra LeRae

Dedication

In Loving Memory of Kim Holmes

11/11/1959 – 09/19/2023

I love and miss you, auntie! I pray you're resting in perfect peace.

Chapter One

Infinity Morrison

I smiled as I pulled up to my job and saw the first parent dropping their child off. While most people dreaded their jobs, I absolutely loved mine. I was a daycare teacher in the infant classroom and had been for the last five years. I looked forward to coming to *Adored Learning* each and every day.

I climbed out of my car and headed toward the entrance. I was met by the director, Ms. Kamille, as she stood to the side allowing the parent and me inside the facility.

"Good morning," I greeted.

"Hey, Infinity. How are you?"

"Good."

I signed in and headed toward my room. The first baby typically didn't come in until closer to seven, but I was going in to get everything set up. It was coming up on Halloween, and I wanted to do a little theme change in the room. I kicked my shoes off before entering my classroom and slid on the slippers I left here strictly for the classroom. Because our babies did a lot of floor play, we had a strict no outside shoe rule when it came to this classroom.

I put my things up and began pulling out the small tables and bouncers. I laid out the freshly washed floor rug and put a few toys on the floor. Once I was done, I headed down to the arts and crafts room to grab a few things I wanted to do with the babies today. I spotted Ms. Kamille at the desk, and she looked stressed. Once I was done grabbing plates, construction paper, paint, and some other things, I stopped by the desk to figure out what was going on with her.

"Hey, are you okay?" I asked.

She sighed heavily. "No, but hopefully, I will be."

"Do you want to talk about it?" I asked.

She shook her head and offered me a small smile. Kamille and I didn't speak outside of work, but she was an amazing boss. I hated that she looked so down. Since she didn't wish to speak about it, I figured it was in her personal life, so I headed back to my classroom. Once I was done setting everything up, I spotted Marissa walking in with her son, Joseph.

"Good morning," I greeted. "Hi, Joey," I smiled as I grabbed him from his mother. I proceeded to take off his coat and handed it to his mom to hang up. I hugged him tight and kissed his cheek. His mother told me his last feeding and diaper change as she unloaded everything from his diaper bag. She handed me a new sleeve of diapers, which I took to put up above our changing area. I placed Joey on the rug, and he instantly crawled and pulled himself up using the bouncer. Joey was eleven months and was ready to take off. His mother smiled as she watched him. She kissed him and then headed out.

It didn't take long before my co-workers, Jasmine and Melanie, came in, as well as a few other children. I noticed today we only had seven babies rather than our normal twelve. Had I not realized that each week for the last few weeks we had been losing children, I wouldn't have paid it any mind. With the count so low, there was no need for three teachers, and while I had been here the longest, it didn't make me any less nervous. I made a mental note to speak to Kamille about enrollment and how it was going.

I explained to Jas and Mel what I wanted to do with the babies for Halloween, and they were down with it. Throughout the morning, we took each baby and made bats, pumpkins, and ghosts for them to take home to their parents. Like clockwork, we had all the babies down and sleeping by noon. I let the girls know that I was taking my lunch break, grabbed my phone, and headed out. I checked my email to see if any of the vacant building owners had reached back out to me. I was in the process of getting my own daycare license to open a daycare. Over the last few months, I asked God to send me signs that this was the right step for me to take. With the noticeable decline in enrollment in the infant room, I was taking that as a sign. There was never a time when the infant room wasn't full along with a waiting list as well.

I was so engrossed in my phone and eating that I didn't hear Kamille come in until she was standing in front of me. I removed an earbud and gave her my attention.

"Hey," I said.

"Can you come see me when you're done eating?" she asked. At that moment, I lost my appetite and my heart dropped into my stomach. To me, it was never a good thing when your boss sought out for you in the middle of the day.

"I can come now," I told her. I closed the lid on what I had for lunch and put it in the fridge in the staff room. I grabbed my water bottle and followed her to her office. She sat behind her desk and put her hands on her head. I was crazy nervous as I sat on the opposite side of her. I wiped my sweaty palms down my pants. "What's going on?"

"Friday is our last day," she notified me.

"Who's last day?"

"Everyone's."

"Huh?"

I just knew I wasn't hearing her correctly. Today was Wednesday, meaning we had two more damn days, and she was letting us all go. Nothing made sense to me.

"I've lost my license. I'm supposed to be closed, but I'm giving notice to parents to allow them to try and find alternative care."

"Wait, what? When did this happen?"

"I got the notice last week. Parents were made aware of the impending closing, which is why enrollment has been going down. I'm sure you've noticed that your class isn't even at half of the capacity." I didn't miss her wiping her face.

"What happened?"

"It doesn't matter. I have to close and that's just that." I sat back in the chair staring at her. I hated being left in the dark, but I knew I couldn't force her to tell me.

"Do the other girls know?"

"I'm letting everyone know today."

"How come we weren't made aware when you found out though? Nobody is going to be able to find a job in two days. That's not fair, Kamille," I complained.

"I can't do anything about it now, Infinity. We have two days left. It's just time to start shutting everything down."

I shook my head and stood to my feet.

"Today is my last day. I have to get started on looking for a new job. Thank you for having me all these years. I wish you all the best." I turned and walked out of her office. I headed back to my infant room to gather all my things together. I kept replaying what just happened.

"You good?" Jasmine asked me. I had to run my tongue across my teeth to keep from shouting and crying. I was hurt that she had to close down, but I was livid that she had known for over a week and didn't bother to say anything. She didn't seem to give a fuck that she was allowing parents to find alternate arrangements but basically said fuck her own employees.

"Kamille will come to talk to y'all, but I'ma tell y'all anyway. She's closing doors Friday," I said.

"Who?"

"Kamille. Friday is the last day of the daycare being open."

"What the fuck?" Melanie stated.

"My thoughts exactly. I told her today is my last day. Shit don't make no damn sense." I shook my head again. The remainder of the day was a blur. A few parents were speaking about the closure when they came into the room, and I couldn't lie, I was sad. I had grown to love all of the babies in my room, and it was sad that our time was being cut short.

At the end of the day, I took a final look at the infant classroom that had grown to feel like a second home to me over the last five years. I shed a few tears before I shut the lights off and closed the door to that part of my life.

Kamille tried talking to me on my way out of the door, but I didn't want to hear anything she had to say. Thankfully, I had been smart and built up my savings account, but my savings were supposed to be for my daycare center. Now I would have to live off of it until I either found a new job or launched this damn business.

One thing was for sure, with the closure of Adored Learning, I was diving headfirst into my own shit and I wasn't stopping until I was opening the doors of *To Infinity and Beyond Learning*

Center.

Chapter Two

Deandre 'Ace' Lemetti

The ringing of my doorbell pulled me from my deep sleep. I had been hitting the streets so fuckin' hard that I rarely slept, but when I did, I crashed and crashed hard. I looked around wondering if what I was hearing was a dream until the person started laying on my doorbell again. Immediately, I got agitated. I grabbed my 9mm out of my nightstand drawer and marched to the front door in nothing but a pair of boxers. Without looking, I opened the door and pointed my gun. My nosey yet cool-ass neighbor, Mrs. Graham, was standing there with her hands up looking scared.

"I-I'm sorry, Ace. I noticed this car seat on your porch and it's kind of chilly this morning." I looked down and almost threw the fuck up. There sat a black and pink car seat along with a diaper bag, two boxes of diapers, and a box of baby wipes taped to the top of it. I felt like my heart was going to explode from my chest.

"I'm sorry, Mrs. Graham. Thank you." I placed my gun on the small table I had behind the door. I bent down and grabbed the car seat and bag. I placed both just inside the door and grabbed the rest of the stuff. "Did you notice who placed it here?" I asked.

"No. I happened to come outside to check my mail and noticed the carrier sitting there."

"Thanks, and again, sorry about that," I said as I closed the door. I grabbed the car seat and walked into the living room. I lifted the flap in the center of the car seat cover and my heart melted. She was absolutely fuckin' gorgeous. She looked just like my sister, Deanna. I placed the seat down and headed back into the foyer to get the envelope off the top of the box. For some reason, I knew this letter was going to piss me clean the fuck off. I took a deep breath as I opened it and unfolded the letter.

Dear Ace,

Let me start off by saying I'm sorry. I really thought that throughout my pregnancy I would change my mind and want to be here, but I don't. I don't and never have seen myself as a mother. I literally only kept her because you begged me to. I will say that pregnancy is a beautiful thing, but babies are way too much work. I tried it out for the last few weeks. She was born on October 10th, at 9:42 am. I'm sorry I didn't tell you about her birth and all of that. I planned on it, but it all happened so fast. I knew our agreement was as soon as she was born, you would take her from the hospital, but I figured I would try to see if it would change my mind. Honestly, it didn't. I thought I may become ready for it, but I'm not.

I didn't name her. The paperwork for her birth certificate is in her diaper bag. I didn't enroll her in medical coverage or anything like that. I figured I would leave that all up to you since she will be with you. I would have handed her directly to you, but I couldn't take the look I know is likely on your face right now. Just know that I tried, Deandre. I really did. Maybe one day both you and her can forgive me. I've included a few pictures in her bag of me while pregnant, as well as the ones I've taken since she was born. Enjoy her. I know you'll take good care of her, just remember to take care of yourself too.

Love,

Liyah

I scanned over the letter several times, hoping it was a damn joke. Aaliyah and I had dated on and off for two years. When she got pregnant, she wanted an abortion, but she was right, I literally begged her not to. I told her if she kept the baby and still didn't want it after she gave birth, I would be a single father. I meant every single word I said, but I definitely thought she would have changed her mind. Aaliyah was very young-minded. She loved to club and drink every damn weekend. I expressed my concerns with her, but at the end of the day, she was an adult.

I was surprised to find the baby on my porch because I had

missed my child's birth and that was something that would piss me off forever. I looked down at my daughter as she slept. I immediately went to my room and grabbed my phone. I FaceTime'd my mother and flipped the camera before she even answered.

"Why are you calling… Oh my God! Whose baby is that?" she questioned.

"Apparently mine."

"What do you mean yours? I just saw you yesterday and you mentioned nothing of a baby."

"It's a long story. Can you come by? I gotta call Deanna. This shit is crazy." I hung up on my mother and dialed my sister.

"What's up, bro?"

"Sis, come to my house ASAP," I told her.

"Everything good?"

"Maybe. Just come on."

I hung up before she could say anything else. Truthfully, I had no idea how to take care of a baby. I was my mother's youngest child, Deanna didn't have kids, and I wasn't around my cousins enough to deal with any of their kids. I was scared to even touch her. She looked so peaceful sleeping that I didn't want to interrupt her.

Less than ten minutes later, my mother barged through the front door with Deanna hot on her heels.

"What the hell is going on?" she asked as she picked the baby up from her car seat. I sighed before I explained the last year of

Aaliyah and my relationship. "What the fuck! So she just gave birth to a child and dumped the child on your porch like last night's trash? Who the fuck even does that! I would say take her to the hospital, but shit, is there even a fuckin' paper trail on this child?" My mother was hot, but I could see the love she was developing for the baby.

"I don't even know."

"What's her name?" Deanna asked.

"She doesn't have one. She wrote a letter. In the letter, it says she left the birth certificate paperwork in the bag, and she didn't name her."

My mother shook her head and sighed. "The bad part is the moment you bring her to the hospital and tell them what happened, they are going to want to determine paternity first before they let you take her."

"Should I do that before I even take her to the hospital?" My mother began undressing her and she stirred in her sleep.

"Yeah. You don't want them to take her from you. Are you sure she's yours?"

"You ain't blind, Ma. You can see she is Deanna's damn twin."

"She really is," Deanna chimed in. "I almost would think she is my child."

"Oh, I already know you're gonna act like she is," I chuckled.

"At least you know. What are you going to name her though?"

"I have no idea," I answered truthfully. I paused for a second and thought about it as I looked at her.

"Gabrielle Deanna Lemetti," I answered.

"Awww," Deanna blushed.

"Deandre, look up a DNA testing center. Ask them how much and how long it takes for a DNA test. We need this ASAP. She looks fine, but I want you to take her to get checked out by a doctor. You also have to submit the birth certificate paperwork as soon as possible," my mother preached.

"I know, I know. I'm trying to take all of this in. I wasn't expecting to wake up to this shit. I had some shit I had to handle today."

"Well, get used to it. Your life now revolves around her. It's time to move smarter and safer. You now have someone relying on you. I'll help you whenever I can, but you gotta make some changes."

"Thanks, Ma."

I walked off to put on some clothes. When I returned, Deanna was on the phone with a DNA testing center and had the appointment already set. The soonest they said they would have it returned would be within twenty-four hours. My mother put the baby back into her car seat and we all piled up in my car and headed to get tested. I couldn't help but keep staring through the rearview mirror at the baby's car seat. I couldn't believe I went from being a single man to a single father in a matter of minutes. I didn't know what this ride was going to bring, but one thing was for sure, I knew it wasn't going to be smooth. However, I was ready for whatever it brought.

Chapter Three

Infinity Morrison

It had been a week since I left my job. The day after, I was approved for my daycare license and registered for my LLC. *To Infinity and Beyond Learning Center* was on the verge of being opened. I hadn't been looking for a job because I was dead set on opening my own daycare. I was pre-approved and had turned in my paperwork for my loan. I was told it may take a few weeks, so I was praying to God daily that everything would work out. My online shopping cart was full and just waiting for me to press purchase. I was ready to fully decorate my daycare center. I put a small deposit down on a place, and just needed my loan to go through to purchase everything. The more I thought about these parents who were left stranded when Kamille closed, the more anxious I got about opening my doors.

I sighed and closed my laptop. I grabbed my clothes to head to the bathroom and take a shower. I hadn't left the house much since leaving my job because I was always working, researching, and turning in the necessary paperwork. Tonight, my cousin and one of my best friends, Danielle, was dragging me out for dinner and drinks. She was tired of me telling her 'not tonight' when she asked me to hang out with her. After how busy the last week had been, I needed a night out.

Within thirty minutes, I was climbing out of the shower. Just as I finished getting dressed, I heard a knock on my front door. I checked the peephole and let Dani in.

"You ain't ready yet?" she asked.

"I just finished getting dressed. Let me brush my hair back and I'm good." I went into my bedroom, grabbed the gel, and created a slick, tight bun. "I'm ready." I grabbed my wallet, phone, and keys, and followed Dani out of the house. "Where are we going?"

"Shaking Crab," she answered.

"Oh! I've been dying to try them," I told her.

"I know. We're calling this a pre-celebration because I know that loan is gonna come through and you're opening your doors soon! I've been manifesting that shit," she cheered. I loved the fuck out of Dani because she was all about positivity and sometimes, that's what I needed.

"I appreciate you," I reminded her. Dani and I laughed and sang together as we headed to Thayer Street. "You know you're going to have to park on a side street because Thayer is always crowded."

"Girl, don't I know it." Thankfully, someone was pulling out of their spot, so we found a parking spot right on Thayer. We walked into the restaurant and were quickly seated. Dani told me to order whatever I wanted because everything was on her.

This night out with Dani was exactly what I needed. It had been so long since we had gone out to do something as simple as dinner and drinks because all I did was work and try and hustle for my business. Several times throughout the night, Dani kept repeating how much she knew my loan was going to come through. I had to start thinking like her because she claimed a lot of shit and the majority of the shit she claimed, came through to her.

*****

Two Weeks Later...

I screamed out loud as I received the approval for my loan. I started dancing around my townhouse, and then I threw myself across my bed and screamed into my pillow. I couldn't believe this was happening. I grabbed my phone and quickly dialed my mother's number.

"Hey, Fin," she answered.

"My loan was approved!" I shouted. "Oh my God! I was approved. I can start setting everything up. I cannot believe this is happening."

"Congratulations, daughter. I'm so proud of you. You deserve all of this. I know your daycare is going to take off!"

"Thank you so much! I cannot stop smiling."

"You deserve it. Bask in your glory then get to work. You have a lot of shopping to do," she sang.

"I know! I gotta call Dani. I'll call you later."

"Alright. I love you and congratulations again."

"Thank you, I love you too." We hung up and I dialed Dani and gave her the news.

"I told you, bitch! I manifested that shit! I'm so proud of you for never giving up. These last few weeks have been tough for you, but you never gave up. Now let's manifest the success. You're about to set it off!"

"Yessss! I have to start hiring and all that other stuff. I want to do an entire grand opening. I have so many ideas!"

"Do all of your ordering of supplies. You already have the building and all of that. You can get your orders delivered as well as post your hiring information online. You have some of the parents from Kamille's daycare on social media, so I'm sure they'll send their kids to you as well. Girl, you have nothing to worry about. Before you know it, you'll be opening a second location."

"I gotta get this one up and running first," I told her.

"You'll be good."

I chatted with Dani for a little while longer before we hung up. I made an appointment to go to the bank to complete any last-minute paperwork. I called the owner of the building and let him know I would be making a few months' rent payments shortly and getting the keys for the location. I had fallen in love with the building. It was small but perfect for what I had planned. I was going to have two infant rooms, two toddler rooms, and two pre-k rooms.

By early afternoon, I had my loan payment and my building keys. I headed to my bank to open a business account and deposit the check. I was still shocked that all of this was happening. When I woke up this morning, I was praying hard, yet I was ending this day as a business owner. This shit was amazing, and I couldn't wait to see my business open and operate.

Chapter Four

Deandre 'Ace' Lemetti

It had been a few weeks since my daughter had been with me. My daughter. The shit still amazed me. We had gotten the DNA results back and proved she indeed was mine. I submitted the birth certificate paperwork and was waiting for her information to come in. My mother told me to be prepared for the state to pop up at my house because there was no mother listed on the paperwork. Until then though, I was getting used to having her around. My mother had taken the last few weeks off of work to help me adjust. I'm not going to lie; it was hard as hell. I was used to jumping whenever I needed to and being out as late as possible, but with Gabby being here, I couldn't do that anymore. Luckily, my nigga Los understood.

My mother had been in my ear about getting her into some sort of daycare because she wasn't always going to be able to watch her. Honestly, after the way her own mother treated her, I was skeptical about letting anyone around her outside of Deanna and my mama. Deanna spoiled her rotten. If she wasn't working, she would be at my house either spending time with her or picking her up. I had always been grateful for my mother and Deanna, but with the way they've stepped up for me recently, I owed them my life.

I had just finished counting the money for the week and was separating it into the duffle bags when my phone started ringing. Looking at the screen, I saw it was my mother. I sighed because I knew she was only calling to give me a lecture, but because Gabby was with her, I wasn't going to ignore her.

"Yeah," I answered.

"Where are you?"

"About to head to pick up Gabby from you."

"How long is it going to take you to get here?"

"I don't know. Maybe like twenty minutes. Why?"

"Because I have shit to do, Deandre! I don't mind helping you with Gabby, especially because I love my grandbaby, but I need you to remember that she's not my child."

"If you don't want to watch her, then just say that," I snapped as I stood and dapped Los up. I grabbed the bag with my cash and headed out. Los was going to pay the workers and put the rest up for our re-up, so I wasn't worried about leaving him alone.

"Is that what I said? No, it's not. What I said was she is not my child. This is an entirely new situation for all of us, but as her parent, you've had it the easiest. Deanna and I have been helping you day in and day out and you're still out here running around like she's not here. You wanted her, Deandre. You have to prioritize. I'm going back to work next week, then what are you going to do?"

"Why can't I just pay you to keep her for me? You know I can pay you more than what that little nursing job you have pays you."

"That's not the point! First of all, I love my job. Second of all, I'm not taking over for you. When you decided to have that girl keep this baby, you told her you would take care of her. It's time that you started doing that. There's more to being a parent than caring for them financially. Now, there's a brand-new daycare that looks to be opening soon. I'll send you the link to the post I saw on Facebook, and you can reach out for information."

"I'm not sending her to no fake ass social media daycare, ma."

"Shut up. It's a legitimate center. Like I said, I'll send it to you. I'll see you when you get here." She hung up before I could say anything else. I shook my head. I listened to everything that my mother had said, and I knew she was telling the truth, but it was hard. For as long as I can remember, I didn't have to care for anyone else. I don't have that story of having to rescue my mom and sister. My mother has been a nurse longer than I can remember. My father was killed in a car accident when I was five, and although it was a blow to our family, my moms never fell off. To me, she had always been, and will always be, superwoman.

It took me fifteen minutes to get to my mother's house. I could see through her bay window that she was sitting in the living room. I threw my car in park and killed the engine before making my way inside. Gabby was dozing off, and I couldn't control the smile that crept across my face. She was absolutely gorgeous, and it was still hard to believe that she was mine.

I leaned over and planted a kiss on my mama's forehead and then on Gabby's cheek. I sat on the opposite couch across from her. I leaned back, took a deep breath, and closed my eyes for a moment.

"What's wrong?" my mama asked.

"So much has changed," I admitted.

"I know. Trust me, I get it. Being a parent is one of the most rewarding yet difficult jobs I've ever had. It seems as if it'll be hard forever, but the good will outweigh the bad." I nodded but didn't respond. "Did you get the link I sent you?" I checked my phone and saw the link she sent. I clicked it and I saw the name of the center was *To Infinity and Beyond Learning Center*. The owner was posting pictures of the setup of the center, from the painting to the furniture, to the kitchen. I tapped on the message button on their Facebook page.

Me: How do I enroll my daughter?

I sent the message and locked my phone.

"I just sent them a message. I'm honestly not sure about this entire daycare thing though. If anything happens to my child, I will lose my shit," I told my mother honestly.

"That's why you do your research. You get a feel for the owner and teachers. Don't just throw her in the first daycare you find."

My phone vibrated on my lap. Checking the notification, I saw that it was the center messaging me back.

To Infinity and Beyond Learning Center: You can come down on Monday for an application. We are slated to open in two weeks.

I responded okay and put the phone back. I let my mother know what they said. I sat and chopped it up with my mother for another two hours before I packed up Gabby in her car seat and headed home. Usually, I stayed at my mother's so she could handle Gabby throughout the night, but again, she was right. I needed to do more on my own for her. After all, she was indeed the child I begged for.

*****

Three Weeks Later...

I strapped Gabby into her car seat as I picked up her diaper bag. Today was the first day of daycare for her, and I couldn't lie, I was scared as fuck. All over the news, you saw news segments about daycare workers abusing children and I swear, I would clear the block behind mine and that was on my life.

It didn't take me long to pull up to the daycare center. When I came last week to enroll her, I got a good vibe from the owner, Infinity. She looked kind of young, but she answered every question that both myself and my mother had for her. Her years of childcare experience sold my mother.

Gabby was awake and looking around. I smiled at her and gave her a kiss on the cheek. I pulled her car seat out of the base and her diaper bag off the floor. I probably overpacked her diaper bag, but I didn't want her to be missing anything.

Walking inside, I saw Infinity sitting behind the check-in desk. She immediately smiled when she saw me. I had to admit, she was a beautiful woman. She looked young as shit, but I could tell that she was a hustla.

"Good morning," she beamed. "This must be Ms. Gabby." She walked around the desk and over to us. "I can walk you down the hall to our infant room," she offered. I nodded and followed behind her. I couldn't help but look at her apple bottom that was filling out her black slacks nicely.

She opened the door and I saw two other women sitting at a table against the wall.

"This is Ms. Jas and Ms. Mel. They are the infant room teachers. Combined, they have more than ten years of childcare experience, especially with infants, so Ms. Gabby will be in great hands."

One thing I could see off the rip with Infinity was her love for children. She wasted no time grabbing the car seat from me and began taking Gabby out of the car seat.

"The sign-in sheet is right here. You just write the time you drop her off, the time you pick her up, and sign your name." I did as she explained and looked at the cubby cubicles for the one with her name before putting her bag inside. I took Gabby from her, removed her jacket, kissed her cheek, and handed her to one of the teachers. I watched as they instantly started smiling and talking to her, and honestly, I felt a sense of calm come over me. Something inside of me let me know that she was in good hands.

I followed Infinity back out to the front of the center.

"So, I noticed the overpacked diaper bag you packed," she chuckled. "You only have to supply her formula, which you can send in pre-separated containers daily, and a few bottles with water, which is easier for the teachers to make the bottles. You can bring a sleeve of diapers at a time and a pack of wipes. Whenever she is running low, we will send a note home in her diaper bag so that you know when to bring more. You can bring one or two outfits for us to keep here just in case there are any accidents. If there are any medications she is on, you can send them in her diaper bag and we will follow the instructions you provide to administer them to her," she explained. "Are there any questions you have?"

"The only question I didn't ask the last time I was here was the cost, which is probably the most important thing," I chuckled.

"Right. The infant rate is $260 per week."

"Damn," I muttered.

"We do accept state daycare vouchers."

"No offense, but does it look like I'm eligible for daycare through the state?" I questioned.

"Honestly, I don't know. I don't base on looks because you never know a person's story."

"Touché," I stated. "When are payments due?"

"Friday at the time of drop off." I nodded in understanding. "Before you go, I just want to check the emergency contact list one more time." She walked around the desk and began running through the drawers. Quickly, she found the paper she was looking for. "So, I have yourself, Deanna Lemetti, and Monique Lemetti. Is that correct?" I nodded and she repeated the numbers that were on the paper for confirmation. "Alright, you are all set. I will see you at pickup time."

She smiled, displaying her deep dimples. I smirked and headed out to handle business for the day.

Chapter Five

Infinity Morrison

As I watched parents come in to drop their children off, it was so surreal. I could not believe my baby was officially opened. I found myself walking from room to room admiring the kids interacting with the teachers and having fun. A time or two I had to go into my office, take a deep breath, and even shed a tear or two. I had waited so long for this, and I had to admit, walking away from Kamille's daycare that day lit a fire under my ass. I talked a lot about opening my own daycare but was dragging my feet at actually doing it. I finally did it, and I couldn't be happier.

From what I had heard, Kamille lost her license due to too many failed inspections. Apparently, there were things in her center that she was advised needed to be updated to meet code standards, and she never did it. It sucked that it cost her, her business, but one thing the state did not play about was code violations, especially in a childcare facility. It was what it was though, and I wished her the best wherever she went from here.

Before I knew it, it was lunchtime. I was in the kitchen helping the kitchen aid load up the lunch trays for the toddler and pre-k rooms. As I rolled the carts down the hall, I couldn't stop smiling. I went into the first room and helped the teacher hand out the lunches. I did the same in the second room. I left the carts outside of the rooms and headed to the front desk. I figured I would use the downtime to start putting the children into the online enrollment system. When I came across Gabrielle Lemetti's folder, I couldn't help but smile. Her father was fine as fuck, I couldn't even front. I was surprised when he walked in the door with the baby. I didn't know his story, but I would be lying if I said I wasn't intrigued. However, I wasn't one to ever mix business and pleasure. Plus, I didn't know what his story was with his daughter's mother, and one thing I didn't like was drama.

I continued inputting the children and answered a few questions that people called regarding enrollment. Before opening, I thought it would take me months to be at capacity, but it was happening quickly. I immediately posted job ads on social media as well as job posting sites for part-time work. Time was flying and without even realizing it, pick-up time was beginning. Just like in the morning, I greeted parents at the door and waved bye to each child who left.

It was fifteen minutes 'til closing and I noticed that Gabrielle was still there. I figured I would give her dad until six before I started calling. At five of six, I watched as his mother came running through the door.

"I'm so sorry. My son called me last minute and I had to leave work early," she said as she rushed through the door. I smiled at her before walking around and leading the way to the baby room.

"It's okay. We don't close until six and I'll give a few minutes before late fees or anything kick in," I explained.

"You can tack those late fees right onto her big head daddy's bill," she said as she chuckled. "This boy is going to be the death of me." I smiled but didn't say anything. I instructed her to kick her shoes off outside of the door. "Hi Nana's baby," she smiled as she picked up a juicy mouth Gabby. The view in front of me brought a huge smile to my face. Gabby's grandmother signed her out before grabbing her bag. I waved to her as she walked down the hall. I pulled out my phone and remotely locked the front door so I could give Jas and Mel a hand in the infant room.

"How was the first day?" I asked.

"Great! I missed this so much and I'm glad you got this center up and running so quickly. My hot little savings I had was quickly dwindling," Mel stated.

"Girl, you ain't never lied," Jas chimed in.

"This shit still doesn't seem real to me," I let them know.

"Girl, bask in this shit. It's yours! Can't nobody fire you. You are the fuckin' boss," Jas shouted. I slapped five with her, grabbed the disinfecting wipes, and proceeded to wipe down the changing table.

"Why are you in here cleaning?" Mel questioned.

"Girl, just because I'm the owner doesn't mean I'm above doing shit like cleaning and taking out the trash. It wasn't long ago that I was an infant teacher myself, so I'm good," I told them. They didn't say anything else. Mel quickly ran the vacuum over the rug before storing it away and the three of us filed out of the room. I went into each room to ensure that all the doors were locked. It was shortly after seven when we were all ready to walk out of the daycare. I activated the alarm and locked the front door. I smiled at my business once more before I walked away and headed home.

Once I made it through the door, I kicked off my shoes, dropped the keys, and closed the door behind me. I went into the kitchen to heat up my leftovers from last night. I grabbed a wine glass and poured myself some wine as my food warmed up. I couldn't help but smile as I thought about the grand opening yesterday.

*****

At the Grand Opening...

Today was the day. The grand opening of my center was here. To say I was nervous would be an understatement. I looked at myself in the bathroom mirror and took a few deep breaths. I smiled, said a silent prayer, and headed out to meet everyone out front. As I stepped out, I saw the ribbon that was stretched out across the front, the news crews setting up, and the city councilwoman who was there to make a speech regarding a new daycare center. My stomach instantly filled with butterflies, and I closed my eyes and took a deep breath. Climbing out of the car, I smiled as I walked towards the front of the building. A small crowd had already formed, and I could hear the cameras clicking as they snapped pictures. Silently, I was telling myself to keep one foot in front of the other so I wouldn't bust my ass in front of all of these people.

I walked up to the councilwoman and shook her hand. I had spoken to her previously when I mentioned opening the center, and she made sure to encourage me, stating our city needed more daycare centers. A news reporter came over to introduce herself as well. I chatted with her as I watched the crowd grow. In the crowd, I saw my mother appear, and I couldn't stop the smile that spread across my face. My mother was my biggest cheerleader, and I knew she wouldn't miss this day if her life depended on it.

Before I knew it, the councilwoman was taking the podium. She started her speech by thanking everyone for coming and speaking on the lack of childcare facilities in the city. She made statements about how she was often notified regarding people not being able to work proper hours due to not having childcare that went around their work hours. I stood there beaming with pride as I was making not only my dreams come true, but helping those parents that truly were in need. A few moments later, it was my turn to speak. Slowly, I walked to the podium and adjusted the microphone.

"Wow," I started, with my voice coming out shaky. I cleared my throat before I continued. "First, I want to thank you all for coming. I have dreamed about this moment for years, and I always talked myself out of taking the right steps to do it. Now, here I am! To start, I want to introduce myself. My name is Infinity Morrison, and I've been a daycare teacher for the last almost six years. I have been working with kids since I was a teenager. I started off babysitting for family members and friends of my mom. Once I graduated high school, I immediately started working for a daycare center.

"A few months ago, that center was shut down. I used that opportunity as motivation to start the process I kept putting off. I won't lie, this was stressful, it was nerve-wracking, and I questioned myself more than I ever have before. I know what I want my center to be, and the thought of failing frightens the life out of me. However, I will do all that I can to be successful and give the children that come through these doors the education and experience of a lifetime.

"I have to thank my mom." I paused and looked at her, offering her a smile. I didn't miss the tears that spilled from her eyes. "She has prayed for me and with me, she has spoken life into my dreams, and she has always, always believed in me. She has always been my voice of reason, and regardless of what

crazy idea I came to her with, she listened without judgment and gave advice wherever she could. I also must thank my best friends, Jasmine and Melanie. We met working at the last daycare center together. They knew of my dreams of eventually opening my own spot. When the last center closed down, they easily could have gone off and found another center to work at. Instead, they patiently waited for me to get through the process and the moment everything was set and ready to go, they jumped on board with no questions asked.

"I also have to thank my community, because without you all, nothing is possible. I promise to love on your babies the same way I would love on my own. I promise to protect your babies. I promise to comfort your babies. I will do everything in my power to bring each and every one of you a sense of relief and safety when you step through our doors. My goal is to make each and every one of you proud of the decision to give us a chance. Ladies and gentlemen, without further ado, I present to you, the To Infinity and Beyond Learning Center." I stepped away from the podium and grabbed the large scissors that the councilwoman was holding. I clipped the ribbon as the crowd broke into a round of applause. I stepped to the side and opened the door, allowing the guests to come in and view the classrooms as well as enjoy the pastries, coffee, and juices that were set out. I had a few parents who quickly asked about enrollment as well as some who asked about job opportunities. I handed out business cards with QR codes for the job applications as well as

paper applications for enrollment.

Two hours later, the crowd had dispersed, and it was just myself, my mom, Mel, and Jas remaining. I smiled as I looked around. I had handed out at least forty enrollment applications and at least seventy-five business cards. We had a set group of children and employees that were starting tomorrow, but I was anxious to see what my business would grow to become.

The beeping of the microwave took me from my thoughts. I smiled widely as I stood to grab my food. I was pulling a page from Dani's book and manifesting nothing but success from my center.

*****

Three Months Later...

I sighed heavily as I looked at my watch. It was a quarter past six and once again, Deandre was late picking up Gabrielle. I let it slide for way too long, but this literally was an almost everyday thing. I felt bad for his mother because she always mentioned how she had to leave work early to rush and pick her up, but she couldn't do it every day because she was going to lose her job.

I picked up the daycare phone again and dialed Deandre's number. I had called his number so damn much lately that I remembered it by heart. I looked over at Gabby who was chewing on a vibrating teething toy while watching TV. Thankfully, Mel and Jas had done a quick run-through of the center so that I wouldn't have to once Gabby left.

"Yo," he answered.

"Mr. Lemetti," I stated firmly.

"Who is this?"

"Your daughter is still at daycare," I told him.

"Oh shit! I'll be there." He hung up before I could say anything else. I sighed and shook my head. Gabby was dozing off, so I took her out of the highchair and cradled her until she fell asleep. A few minutes later, my phone vibrated with my center outdoor camera letting me know that someone was at the door. I shut the TV off and grabbed Gabby's bag as I headed to the front of the center. Opening the door, he rushed inside and immediately grabbed Gabby from me.

"My bad, man. I got caught up with work."

"Can I talk to you?" I asked him.

"I said my bad," he snapped.

"Mr. Lemetti, this is becoming an everyday thing. We must find something that'll work for everyone, so I'm not stuck here late all the time or your mother rushing from work to get her. I was thinking-."

"Yo, don't tell me you're one of those that try and call the people on muthafuckas," he said, cutting his eyes at me.

"What? No. If I was going to call *the people*, as you call it, I would have done it a long time ago. I want to help you."

"Help me? Help me how?"

"Listen," I sighed, shifting my weight from one foot to the other. "I've been working with kids my entire adult life. If you give me permission, I'm willing to take Gabby home with me at the end of the day until you're done doing what you gotta do."

"What? The fuck you trying to kidnap my kid or some shit?" I didn't miss his nostrils flare and the vein in his forehead started to pulse.

"Can you chill out?" I spat. "I can see that you're a new father. Raising kids ain't easy. I don't have kids, but I've watched people struggle, and I hate to see it."

"So what are you trying to say?"

"If you shut up for one second and listen, I can get to the point, Mr. Lemetti."

"Stop beating around the damn bush, Miss Infinity." I had to pause and close my eyes for a second because the way my name rolled off of his tongue did something to me just that fast. His voice was deep. For a split second, I pictured him whispering in my ear and I shuttered. "You good?"

I opened my eyes and realized I had zoned out for a second. I took a deep breath and looked at him shifting his daughter from one arm to the other.

"With your permission, I will take her with me at the end of the day. I'll get her situated for the evening; dinner, bath, bed, all the good things, depending on what time you plan on picking her up. I'll give you my address and my phone number for you to have so you can call or whatever."

The space between us became quiet and I felt like I could hear my heart beating in my ears. For the first time, I felt like I had overstepped my boundaries and he probably thought I was doing way too much. Truth be told, during the times that Gabby and I stayed late, I had gotten used to her. Sometimes we played with toys, we played peek-a-boo, watched cartoons, or I simply held her and stared into her eyes. She was such a beautiful little girl and despite her dad and his late pickups, I could tell she was very well taken care of.

"A'ight," he responded. I bucked my eyes a little bit because I thought I was hearing things. I had never done anything like this before, but for some reason, I was willing and wanted to do anything I could to help Deandre. "Don't try no funny shit with my daughter."

"I would never," I assured him. "It seems like you have a lot on your plate and outside of your mom, you seem to be tryna do everything on your own."

"Shit's been wild if I'm being honest. I appreciate you tryna help a nigga though. I'm sure it'll relieve some stress from my mom dukes' shoulders."

"Where's her mother?" I asked as I noticed Gabby starting to wake up. She looked at her dad, gave him a small smile, and placed her head back on his shoulder. For a six-month-old, Gabby was on the move. She was already trying to pull herself up onto objects to stand up and she crawled like a champ.

Deandre looked at Gabby, planted a kiss on her cheek, and looked back at me.

"That's a story for another day, Miss Infinity." There it was again.

"Please, drop the Miss and just call me Infinity."

"Only if you promise to call me Ace. My mama is the only one that calls me Deandre and I hate it," he smiled, showing off his perfectly white, straight teeth.

"Deal."

"I appreciate you, Ma. For real. This is all new for a nigga like me and I'm still adjusting."

"No problem. Have a good night."

"Are you gonna give me your number first?" he questioned as he pulled his phone out of his pocket.

I smirked as I took the phone from him and plugged my number in.

"Have a good night," I repeated.

"You too."

I watched as he and Gabby walked out and headed toward his car. I couldn't drop the smile that was on my face and smiled so hard, that I thought my cheeks would burst. I didn't know Deandre's story, but something inside of me made me want to help him get through this journey of fatherhood.

Chapter Six

Deandre 'Ace' Lemetti

I sat and watched as Gabby kicked her feet and splashed in her baby bathtub. I still couldn't believe I had a daughter, and I couldn't front, the shit was hard tryna be a father to her and handle my shit in the street. The street shit paid bills and allowed me to take care of my daughter. My mother was in my ear heavily about letting the street shit go, and it sounded good, but the money was greater. I wasn't a nigga that touched work. I wasn't a kingpin, but I had my own crew that got their hands dirty for me. I oversaw everything and counted the money. Money was coming in so fast, that I've been doing counts almost daily.

It was never my intention to leave my daughter late at daycare. My mom agreed to pick her up, but most of the time she sends me texts at the last minute, and I don't see the shit until it's too late.

When Infinity approached me with her proposition, I was skeptical as fuck. I didn't know this girl from a hole in the wall, but the fact that outside of doing her job, she still wanted to help was a turn-on for me. All Gabby had was me, Deanna, and my mother. My mother and Deanna did what they could, but I didn't expect them to raise Gabby. For the most part, I was trying to figure this shit out on my own.

I grabbed Gabby out of the tub and started kissing her cheek, causing her to giggle. Her laugh did something to a nigga's heart. I knew whenever I had children I would love them, but I never imagined the love being this strong. This shit was wild.

It didn't take much time at all before Gabby was asleep. I laid her in her crib, grabbed the baby monitor, and headed toward my living room. Plopping on the couch, I grabbed my stash of weed and rolled a blunt. Fatherhood was different. I loved every moment of it, but it also made me grow newfound respect for mothers, single mothers at that because this shit was not for the weak. A nigga like me came and went as I pleased, but with Gabby, that shit didn't happen like that. There was no more just up and running out. There was no more partying for days straight. Everything revolved around Gabrielle. I sparked up my blunt and turned on the TV. I turned on the sports highlights and kicked my feet up on the ottoman. I pulled out my phone and decided to send Infinity a text.

Me: (8:54 PM) - *What's good with you?*

My mother was calling me before I could even put the phone

down.

"Yeah," I answered.

"What time did you get to the daycare?" she questioned.

"A little after six."

She sighed heavily. "You have got to do better, Deandre. The daycare closes at six. There is no reason why you are late."

"Is this what you called me for?"

"I'm just now leaving work and saw the missed calls from the daycare from earlier," she explained. My mother was an ER nurse, and she was always pulling twelve-hour shifts.

"It shouldn't be an issue moving forward though. She offered to help me."

"What you mean?" I went on to explain the deal that Infinity made me. "You don't even know the girl."

"Come on, Ma. She owns and runs the daycare Gabby has been going to for months. One thing I do know about her is she cares about my kid. Unfortunately, my line of work does not have dedicated hours, so there may be times I can't make it to the daycare on time."

"Bullshit. You just have a bad sense of timing. You don't pay attention to the time when you're out."

"I can't always focus on the time. Sometimes there is shit that requires a lot of my time."

"Whatever. If something happens to my baby, that's your ass, Deandre."

"Yeah, yeah. How was work?" I asked her, changing the

subject.

"It was work. You know the ER is always busy, so it's nonstop. I'm glad that I'm off tomorrow. I'm sleeping in," she said. I chuckled because I knew she wasn't lying. It was likely that she was going to shut her phone off and keep her room darkening shades closed all day.

"A'ight, well get home and get some rest. I love you."

"I love you too." Just as the call ended, my phone vibrated, alerting me of a text. Checking my messages, I saw it was a response from Infinity.

Infinity: (9:03 PM) – *Who is this?*

I smirked as I responded.

Me: (9:04 PM) – *Ace*

Almost immediately, my phone started ringing. I was surprised to see Infinity calling me rather than responding to the text.

"Hello."

"Is everything okay with Gabby?" she asked.

"Yeah, why would something be wrong?"

"I wasn't expecting a text from you, especially this late."

"Nah, I was just trying to see what you were up to, that's all."

"Oh." The phone became quiet. "Nothing. Getting ready for bed."

"Am I interrupting you?"

"No, not really."

"Are you nervous?"

"W-why would I be nervous?"

I chuckled. "Just the vibe I'm getting. You seem like you don't want to talk though, so I'll let you go."

"Oh okay, then."

I ended the call and chuckled again as I finished smoking my blunt. I had to feel Infinity out a little bit more to be able to talk to her outside of dealing with Gabby. It was something about her that I was interested in getting to know, but I could tell it would probably take some time to get to know her...the real her.

Chapter Seven

Infinity Morrison

I looked at the phone sideways when I heard the three beeps in my ear, indicating he had hung up. When I read the message that it was him, my heart immediately started racing. My initial thought was something was wrong with Gabby, so that's why I called. Hearing his voice come through the phone had me back in that place I was in earlier, where I was squeezing the fuck out of my thighs. I closed my eyes and pictured his lips. Those fuckin' lips. They were nice and full, and they looked super soft. I pulled my bottom lip in between my teeth. I tossed myself back on the bed and groaned. I couldn't believe I had him on the phone and clammed up like a teenager.

I grabbed my phone and dialed Jas up quickly.

"Hey boo," she answered on the third ring.

"He text me."

"Huh?"

"He text me," I repeated.

"He who?"

"Ace."

"Who the hell is Ace?" I laughed because I realized that I hadn't told her what I agreed to earlier today.

"Gabrielle's father."

"Gabrielle as in the baby at the daycare?"

"Yes."

"Wait, back the fuck up. When did you even give him your personal number?"

I ran down the discussion and agreement that we made earlier, which led to me giving him my number.

"Well alright then, bitch! Gon' ahead and get your groove back. It's been long enough."

She wasn't lying. I hadn't dealt with anybody in years. Once I left my ex, I said fuck a relationship and focused on busting my ass to open my daycare. I'm not going to lie, that relationship traumatized the fuck out of me.

"Girl, it ain't nothin'."

"Yet."

"Whatever."

"Let's keep it real, Fin. You just called me crazy excited that the nigga texted you. You definitely feeling him."

"I don't even know him."

"But you can get to know him. Anyway, what did he say when he texted you?"

"Honestly, I initially thought something was wrong with Gabby, but he told me she was good, and I clammed up like a fuckin' teenager," I sighed. "I feel like I don't even know how to hold a conversation with a dude outside of work," I admitted.

"Call him back," she suggested.

"Not after the way I just acted."

"You'll have more than one opportunity to make up for this first time. Just be you, Fin. Not every nigga is like Jermaine." Just the mention of my ex made me roll my eyes.

"Let's not even discuss his asshole," I mentioned, wanting to immediately change the subject. I chatted with Jas for a little while longer before we ended the call. I stared at my phone, tempted to call Ace back, but decided against it. Instead, I scrolled through my DVR and put on *Marriage Bootcamp: Hip Hop Edition.* It wasn't long before I was dozing off.

*****

I pulled into the parking lot of the center shortly after six in the morning. I grabbed my coffee and tote bag and exited the vehicle. I couldn't stop the smile that graced my face. My heart started racing. The site of my center always brought a sense of happiness over me. It still seemed unreal that this was actually mine.

I unlocked the door, entered, and locked the door again behind me. The doors opened at six thirty, but the first child usually didn't show up until after seven. Jas and Mel will be here shortly. I entered my office and booted up my computer. I planned on checking my Facebook messages and email for any new enrollment inquiries. I wasn't going to lie, I was shocked as hell that the spots were filling up as quickly as they were. Luckily, I was able to gather a few of the kids who Kamille left high and dry, but word of mouth and advertising also brought me in more kids.

I also made a mental note to see if I had any new job applications. With the way the enrollment was filling out, I knew I would need to hire more people. I slipped my feet out of my flats and logged into the system. I sipped my coffee as everything loaded, and I was surprised to see five new applications for hiring. I squealed and did a little dance in my seat as I began reading over the applications and jotting down numbers to call and set up interviews. I even had an applicant for the front desk.

Before I knew it, the bell at the door was ringing. Glancing at my phone, I saw it was Jas and Mel, so I electronically unlocked the door for them to come in.

"Morning, boo," Jas greeted as they both appeared in the doorway.

"Hey!"

"Did you call your boo back?" she asked. I rolled my eyes because I knew she was not going to let this go.

"He's not my boo," I said throwing a paperclip at her.

"Whatever." Mel looked lost so I quickly filled her in.

"I say go for it. If it doesn't work out, then it doesn't work out, but it doesn't hurt to try."

"Y'all act like this nigga asked me out on a date. All he did was text me." I rolled my eyes.

"Girl, the nigga text you late night. Muthafuckas don't do that just because. You can keep playing dumb if you want. You already agreed to help the nigga with his kid, it's only a matter of time before he's wining and dining you."

"Help with his kid?" Mel kept looking back and forth between me and Jas. I proceeded to explain the deal I made with Ace to help a little more with Gabby. "Oh yeah, he's gonna end up wifing your ass."

"I swear y'all are so extra," I laughed. They both left out of my office and headed down to their classroom. Like clockwork, the first child arrived at seven on the dot, as well as the remainder of the staff members. Soon, we were in full swing of morning drop-offs. My phone vibrated in the pocket of my slacks, so I looked at my Apple Watch and saw it was a text from Ace. I immediately tried to stifle the smile, but it wasn't working. My cheeks instantly began to hurt.

Ace (7:54 AM): Good morning. What kind of coffee do you like?

I began chewing on my bottom lip as my fingers started typing my response.

Me (7:55 AM): I've already had my coffee today but thank you.

I sent the message before letting another parent in the door. I greeted them and sat behind the desk. My phone vibrated again. Lifting my left wrist, I read Ace's response.

Ace (7:57 AM): That's not what I asked and I'm not a fan of repeating myself, Miss Infinity.

I chuckled and shook my head as I sent him my coffee order. Shortly after eight, I saw Ace walking down the walkway with Gabby in one hand and a coffee from Dunkin' in the other. I dropped my head as I felt myself blushing like a schoolgirl.

"Now I know good and damn well your ass was watching the camera and saw me, so don't try and act like you didn't," I heard his voice boom the moment the door opened. I smirked and blushed again as I walked around the desk to greet him.

"Good morning, Mr. Lemetti."

"Ace. Mr. Lemetti was my father," he corrected. I playfully rolled my eyes and chuckled. "This is for you." He handed me the Dunkin' cup.

"I told you I already had a coffee."

"And I told you that wasn't what I asked. You're dealing with kids all day. I know you'll need more than one cup of coffee a day."

I smiled and dropped my head. I felt him cup my chin and direct my head back up.

"Don't do that," he said looking into my eyes. "Your smile is beautiful. Don't try to hide it, especially from me." I lowered my eyes. This man was doing something to me. He was awakening parts of me that had been sleeping for years. "Look at me," he demanded. His voice was calm but demanding. Looking into his brown eyes had me in a trance. He smirked, and I almost went weak in the knees. I took a step back, closed my eyes, and took a deep breath.

"Thanks again for the coffee," I said. I had to get away from this man. He had me ready to risk it all and allow him to bend me the fuck over my desk.

"You ain't ready for all that," he chuckled. "No problem though."

He winked as he headed down to the infant room to drop Gabby off. I sat my ass behind the desk and took a few deep breaths. The seat of my panties was moist, and I had to press my thighs together. I bit my bottom lip and tried to push the freaky thoughts in my head away.

"Whatever it is you're thinking about me doing to you, all you gotta do is say the word, and I'll make it all happen."

I jumped slightly as I opened my eyes and stared at Ace and his cocky-ass smile. My heart was racing, and I was now afraid to stand up because I would be lying if I said that I didn't get a little wetter.

"Just let me know when you're ready to stop playing," he winked and walked out of the center. My eyes followed him until I could no longer see him. I immediately picked up my phone and shot a text to both Jas and Mel.

Me (8:17 AM): This man is going to get me in trouble, and I honestly don't know if I'm against it.

I locked the daycare door and headed into my office to start making calls to set up interviews. I received the notification that additional requests for enrollment were coming in. I couldn't stop the smile that was spreading across my face. Soon, I was going to have to have a waiting list. My vibrating phone broke me from writing.

Jas (8:41 AM): If Stella can get her groove back, then you can too.

I chuckled and put the phone back down. For the next few hours, I made phone calls, set up meetings, visited classrooms, and took pictures to post on our Facebook page. Just as I was heading into the kitchen to help prepare lunch, my phone vibrated. I lifted my wrist to check my watch and was surprised to see Kamille texting me. I hadn't heard from her since I left her center months ago.

Kamille (12:09 PM): I see you've got your center up and running. I love it. I'm happy for you. I'm sorry about the way I let everyone know about me losing my license, but truthfully, I was embarrassed. I had my center for years, and in the blink of an eye, I was losing it. I pray you have many years of success with your center. It looks amazing.

I had to read the message twice because when I saw her name, I initially thought she was going to talk shit. I had spoken several times to Kamille about my dreams of one day being where she was with owning her childcare center. I pulled my phone out of my pocket and thanked her for her kind words before wishing her well. Before I could put it back, it began ringing. I smirked when I saw Ace's name.

"Hello," I answered.

"What's up? What you doing?"

"Ummm, working," I responded. "What else would I be doing during the middle of the day?"

"A'ight, you got that smart ass. How's my baby girl?"

"She's good." I shifted and placed the phone between my ear and shoulder as I started loading the lunch carts.

"You busy?" he questioned.

"I'm loading the lunch carts for the toddler rooms," I told him.

"What are you doing for lunch?"

"Probably order some Asian Chili wings from 148 or something. I'm not sure," I let him know.

"A'ight bet."

"Will you be on time today to pick up Gabby?" I questioned.

"Yeah."

"Okay."

"I was just checking on you though. I'll holla at you later," he said and disconnected the call. I smiled as I put my phone back in my pocket.

"I haven't seen a grown woman blush that hard in a long time," the cook, Ms. Moe stated. I chuckled and shook my head as I placed the gallon of milk on the cart and grabbed some plastic cups. I didn't say anything as I headed out of the kitchen and toward the rooms to deliver lunch. By the time I made it back to the front desk, I saw a gentleman standing outside the door with a bag. I twisted my face as I made my way over. I cracked the door open before speaking.

"Hi, can I help you?" I questioned.

"I have a delivery for Infinity," he responded.

"From who?"

"I just was told to pick this up from 148 and deliver it here to Infinity," he shrugged. I opened the door a little wider to grab the bag from him. "Have a good day." He walked away before I could say anything else. I stood there stuck, but I couldn't stop the smile that graced my face. I went back inside and locked the door behind me. I went into my office, opened the bag, and chuckled as I pulled out my phone. I tapped on Ace's name and put the phone on speaker.

"Yo," he answered.

"You didn't have to."

"I wanted to. Now enjoy your lunch and I'll see you when I get there to grab Gabby." He ended the call again before I could say anything else. I sat back in my chair and stared at the bag. Before I could dig in, Jas was standing in the doorway.

"Why didn't you tell me you were ordering something?" she questioned as she popped a seat in the chair across from me.

"Because I didn't order it." She twisted her face as I chuckled. I told her about the message that Ace sent and the food delivery.

"Nah, tell Mr. Man that if he's going to be ordering lunch, he needs to make sure that we ain't hungry too," she joked. I laughed and slid the container over to her as she wasted no time digging in. We made small talk as we ate some of the wings. I saved some in case Mel didn't bring lunch.

For the remainder of the day, I did my normal routine around the center, and before I knew it, it was pickup time. When Ace hadn't shown up by five of six, I shut everything down and headed out the door to take Gabby home with me. He could tell me whatever he wanted, but the only thing he was ever on time for was drop-off. I didn't mind though. I love me some Gabby.

Chapter Eight

Deandre 'Ace' Lemetti

By the time I plugged my phone in, my heart instantly hit the floor when I saw it was a quarter to seven. I was expecting a flood of messages from Infinity cursing me out. Instead, I had one lone text that let me know she had Gabby and to let her know when I was on the way. I sat back and washed my hands over my face. I knew right now Infinity didn't seem to have an issue with helping with Gabby, but I didn't want her to think I was taking advantage of her.

I shifted the car into drive, tapped her name, and put the phone on speaker. The phone rolled over to voicemail, so I ended the call and called her back. I was met with the same result. I stopped at the liquor store and grabbed a bottle of wine and a bottle of 1738. It was Friday night, and I wanted to give her a small token of appreciation for all the help she had been giving with Gab. When I came out, I spotted an older Spanish man standing on the corner selling flowers. I dropped my bottles in the car, walked over, and purchased two bouquets.

I tried to dial Infinity's number again but was still getting her voicemail. I dropped the phone into the cup holder and headed toward her townhouse. I expected her to call me back during that time, but she didn't. When I pulled up outside of her house, I spotted her car in its normal parking spot with the lights on in her townhouse. As I walked by her car, I dialed her number again and saw her cupholder light up. I chuckled as I realized she had left her phone in the car and probably didn't even notice it. I saw her car door was unlocked, so I opened the door to grab her phone before knocking on her door.

I could hear her TV on cartoons and Gabby cooing. I smiled as I heard Infinity's voice.

"Who could that be, Gabby? Let's go see who is at the door." I heard her make the kissing noise, followed by Gabby's giggling. She opened the door and I stood there with the flowers and wine. "Hey," she greeted, stepping to the side. I stepped inside and Gabby immediately started calling out for me.

"Da-da. Da-da."

"Uh-uh! Don't call for him, Gabby," Infinity said, hugging Gabby closer.

"You left this in your car," I told her, holding up her phone.

"Damn, I didn't even realize."

"I figured that after I called you several times." I dropped it on the table. "I wanted to grab these for you as a thank you, though." I handed her the flowers. "I appreciate all of the help you do with Gabby and do it without any complaints."

"Aww, thank you. You didn't have to though. I've grown to love this little girl." She nuzzled her nose into Gabby's neck, tickling her in the process.

"That's the shit right there that makes a thug feel kinda mushy," I stated. "The way you are with her means a lot to a nigga, for real."

"You feeling okay? I never thought I would see the day that Mr. Lemetti would be all soft and shit," she chuckled.

"Get to know me and you'll learn a lot of new things. I'm not sure what kind of wine you like, but this is one that I know my mama liked so I figured I would grab it for you," I said, holding the bottle out. She took the bottle from me just as Gabby reached out for me.

"I've never had it," she said staring at it. "I'll give it a try though. You want a glass too?"

"I grabbed myself a bottle of Remy. If you have a shot glass or something, it'll be cool."

She placed the bottle on her coffee table and headed into the kitchen.

"I was just about to mix the spaghetti I was making," she called out. "Do you want a plate?"

"Sure."

"Feel free to strip Gabby down to her diaper and put her in the highchair that's in the corner."

Looking to my right, I noticed she had a highchair in the corner. I couldn't help the smile that graced my face. Gabby started clapping her hands when she realized I was sitting her in her chair.

"When did you grab this stuff?" I asked.

"What stuff?"

"Highchairs and shit."

"Shortly after I started helping you. Initially, I didn't have anything, but realized she needed toys, a place to sit and eat, and sleep."

"How much was it?"

"Don't worry about it."

I looked toward the kitchen where she was before I stripped Gabby to place her into the highchair. When I had her in the seat, I pulled money from my pocket and peeled off three one-hundred-dollar bills before tucking them on the side of her cable box. I knew she didn't ask for me to pay her, but I damn sure didn't want her feeling like she was obligated.

"Is she old enough to eat spaghetti?"

"I've been doing research on something called baby-led weaning, which is basically like instead of feeding baby food, you feed them table food. She's almost eight months old, so I've been trying easy to mash things. We've tried a few fruits and veggies, which she likes. Her favorite ironically is steamed broccoli. She gets super messy, but that, followed by some fruit she chews through her mesh pacifier, and a bottle and she's out like a light. I don't do it every day I have her, but when I do, she enjoys it."

"Well damn. Thanks for letting me know. Almost seems like you know more about my child than I do," I joked as I watched her put a few pieces of broccoli on her tray with a few strands of spaghetti noodles. She set the little pacifier-looking thing next to her with what looked like an orange slice inside. Gabby smiled before digging right in. Infinity walked back to the kitchen once she realized that Gabby was all set with her food. She came back with a plate for both of us. The moment I spotted the plate, my stomach growled loudly, reminding me I hadn't eaten all day. I couldn't lie, a nigga was happy to be getting a home-cooked meal. Between running the streets and keeping up with Gabby, it was rare I cooked. Since my mama often worked late, there was no getting a plate from her.

"Do you want parmesan cheese?" she asked. I nodded but was already digging in before she could even go and get it. The shit was amazing, and I already knew I was going to need another plate after this one. "Damn, slow down," she laughed. "There's more if you want seconds."

"I appreciate it, ma." She placed the grated cheese on the table along with a wine glass for herself and a shot glass for me. She turned the TV on, and we ate in silence. I glanced at Gabby and noticed she had sat back and was drinking her bottle, looking like she was getting tired. Infinity noticed too, so she placed her plate down before walking around and grabbing her out of the chair.

"I'll be right back."

"You don't have to do that. I can get ready to head home."

"I'm enjoying your company," she admitted. "I'll just wipe her down really quickly and put her in pajamas. She'll be out soon."

I sat back and thought about how much Infinity knew about Gabrielle. She seemed interested in knowing and doing as much as she could for her, and it made me wonder how Aaliyah could walk away from it without a second thought.

In less than ten minutes, she came back with Gabby in her pajamas. She was rubbing her eyes and instantly reached out for me. I grabbed her and laid her on my chest as I leaned my head back against the back of the couch. I closed my eyes for a second and felt the opposite side of the couch sink.

"Can I ask you something?" I asked, never opening my eyes.

"Sure."

"You're amazing with Gabby, and it's clear you love and adore kids. Have you ever considered having your own?"

I felt her shift on the couch and clear her throat. I peeked out of my eye and realized she looked extremely uncomfortable. She began fiddling with her fingers.

"I'm sorry. Was that too personal?" I questioned.

"I-it's fine. I've just never spoken about it before." She cleared her throat again and sniffled. "I-I don't know if I can have kids." I scrunched my face in confusion.

"What would make you think that?"

She took a deep breath and closed her eyes. I sat up and laid a sleeping Gabby on the couch next to me.

"If it's too deep, Ma, you don't have to answer it. I was truly just curious. Kids are not for everyone."

"It's not that. There's nothing more that I want than a child." She sighed heavily before speaking again. "My ex and I split four years ago. He couldn't be faithful if his life depended on it." She chuckled and shook her head. "Shortly after we split, I found out that I was eight weeks pregnant. I wanted absolutely nothing to do with him, so I never told him about my pregnancy or the baby," she paused and cleared her throat again. "The start of my pregnancy was great. The baby was growing healthy and had me glowing like crazy. Nobody could tell me anything," she chuckled and sniffled. "When I was twenty-two weeks, I woke up covered in blood. I rushed to the emergency room, and they told me my placenta had ruptured and I had to deliver the baby. I was scared shitless. They told me I had no choice but to deliver, and I knew at twenty-two weeks, there was no chance of my baby surviving. My plan had always been to deliver naturally, but an emergency c-section was performed, and during the process, they tore my stomach up. From the way the doctor explained it, they pretty much shredded everything trying to get the baby out.

"They told me if I ever were to get pregnant again, my cervix wouldn't be strong enough to withhold a full pregnancy.

Unfortunately, my son had no chance at survival, and in the process, the surgeons seemed to have stripped my ability to have future children. The worst part about it is that they didn't even seem apologetic about it. They wanted me to look at the bright side that they saved my life." She shook her head. "It seems like that day I lost my son and part of my womanhood. I thought it would be hard going back and working with children again, but my babies at the daycare brought me a sense of peace. They helped me through many of the days that I wanted to curl into a ball and die. Something about when I laid eyes on Gabby, brought me a new feeling. I still don't know what it is about her, or you, that made me want to go the extra mile, but I'm glad I did. Throughout the last few months, I fell in love with this precious little girl. She gave me hope that one day, I might actually get the chance to be a mother. Either way though, whether I can or can't, Gabby filled a void that was empty for a long time."

I was speechless. I wasn't expecting her to dump that on me, but it seemed as if it released a weight she had been carrying for a long time.

"You're strong, Ma. Stronger than many others, and never feel like you're not. I'm sorry for the loss of your son. Always know though, that God has the final say. No child will ever replace your son, but I know when the time is right, you will be blessed," I told her.

"Look at you, being all religious and shit," she laughed.

"Nah," I chuckled. "I don't go to church and none of that, but I do believe in the man above, and that He is the one with the final say. If anybody deserves a child, it's you. If I could give my daughter a new mother, I definitely would. I'm glad she's here though, and although the way I got her was crazy as fuck, I wouldn't trade it for the world," I explained.

"Thank you. Sorry for unloading my trauma on you. I haven't spoken about my son to anybody in a long time, and it actually felt good to speak about him."

"Did you bury him?"

"No, I cremated him. His urn sits on my nightstand, so I talk to him often."

"What was his name?"

"Bentley Josiah Morrison."

"Infinity and Bentley," I laughed.

"Shut up."

The space between us became quiet.

"Tell me about Gabby's mother," she said. I sighed heavily as I sat back and stared at the wall ahead before opening up about my relationship with Aaliyah. I vowed to never speak on the woman again, but she opened up to me, there was no way I couldn't open up to her.

Chapter Nine

Infinity Morrison

I sat and stared at Ace while he looked at the wall. It had been so long since I talked to anyone about Bentley, but I would be lying if I said I didn't feel good about it. Every day I prayed to God and my son to allow me to experience motherhood, but I accepted that it may not ever happen.

Ace sighed and shook his head.

"Aaliyah and I were together for a few years. I was doing my thing and taking care of her. She was the one I planned on spending my life with. I didn't expect anything from her honestly, just loyalty. I started talking about starting a family with her. She acted like she was down with it, but the moment she actually found out she was pregnant, that shit changed. She then became upset she would have to give up her party ways," he sighed heavily. "I begged her not to get an abortion. I told her if she kept the baby and decided she still didn't want it, I would raise the baby by myself. The next thing I knew, she had disappeared. She changed her number, blocked me on all social media, and was not staying with anybody I knew she hung out with. I searched high and low for her ass for months and got nothing. Then, seven months ago, I woke up to someone banging on my door. I open the door and my neighbor is there with a baby on the porch." He shook his head and washed his hands down his face. "She left my fuckin' baby on the porch with a blank birth certificate and a damn letter."

My heart dropped. Here I was yearning to be a mother and this lady would rather party than being there for her child. I couldn't help but shake my head.

"She doesn't know what she's missing. Gabby is amazing," I said looking at her sleeping. "How does it feel raising her?"

"It's the hardest shit I've ever had to do in my life," he laughed. "But honestly, I wouldn't have it any other way. I know I've fucked up since I've had her, and I'm sure I'll fuck up a million more times, but to watch her grow, the shit is amazing. I just wish her mother was around to see it."

The room became quiet between the two of us. I mainly saw Gabby during the daycare center and the few hours I had her after, and I couldn't even begin to understand how anybody could walk away from such a good baby.

"You're a blessing to her. There is no book on parenting, so just like every other parent, you'll make mistakes. As long as you do the best you can and you're not putting her in harm's way, you'll be good," I smiled as I patted his knee.

He looked at me and smiled.

"Tell me about yourself," he said, sitting back on the couch. I noticed he kicked off his fresh wheat Timbs.

"What do you wanna know?"

"Whatever you want to tell me. I should know more about the lady who has my child just as much as me," he chuckled. I shrugged.

"There isn't much to me. I'm twenty-four and I own the daycare center."

"How long have you worked with children?"

"Since I was sixteen. I started babysitting young and when I graduated high school, I started working at the daycare center I was at before they closed."

"Why did they close?" he sat up and poured himself another shot.

"Apparently, she had too many failed inspections. I wish she had said something because I would have done anything I could to help her. It is what it is though," I shrugged.

"You wasn't worried about what would happen?" he asked, taking his shot to the head.

"Of course, but I talked so much about opening my center that I felt like that was why God had me losing my job. I needed to stop putting it off. I decided at that moment to go ahead and get the ball rolling. I did a lot of praying to get it done and it came full circle for me," I smiled.

"That's what's up, ma. You don't see many young people as business owners or even really knowing what it is they wanna do. You got that shit figured out. I respect it."

"Thank you. What about you?"

"What about me?" he asked, pouring another shot.

"Tell me about yourself."

"Shit, I'm just a straightforward type of nigga. I'm twenty-eight. My mama raised me and my sister as a single mother after my father died. I mean I know it ain't hard to tell what I do, so yeah," he shrugged. I knew what he was getting at, and I wasn't about to judge him. On these streets, sometimes you had to do what you had to do.

"Do you plan on doing that forever?"

"Nah, not at all. I want to actually live to see Gabby grow up, and in this lifestyle, the usual way out if you don't get out in time, is either dead or in jail, and I'm not tryna end up in either spot."

"How is your relationship with your sister?" I asked, pouring myself another glass of wine.

"She's my best friend. She also acts like she is my second mother, but I wouldn't trade her for the world. She's pretty dope sometimes," he responded.

"Just sometimes?"

"Yeah, other times she's corny and annoying," he laughed.

Ace and I sat and talked for another two hours. I hadn't even realized how much time had passed until he mentioned it.

"Let me get Gabby home and in bed. I enjoyed myself tonight. I appreciate you letting me get to know you, and hopefully, this isn't the last time you allow me in your personal presence." He smiled at me as he slid his foot into his boots. I smirked and grabbed Gabby, putting her sweater on before placing her into her seat. I buckled her in, adjusted her straps, and picked her up. "Nah, you've done more than enough for us tonight. I got her."

"Can you let me know when you make it home safe?" I asked him.

"I got you." He stepped toward me and planted a kiss on my forehead. I damn near melted at the feeling of his lips.

"Drive safe."

"Will do."

I watched from my doorway as he clicked Gabby into her base and climbed into the car. I waved and closed the door once he pulled off. I headed up to my bedroom and stripped down to take a quick shower. I couldn't stop smiling. Ace was like a breath of fresh air. It was nice getting to know him on a personal level, and one thing I could say was Gabby had a loving dad in her life. I meant what I told him. Being around Gabby gave me hope that I would one day be blessed with my own child.

*****

Two Weeks Later…

I spun around in my room as I sang along to Beyonce's *End*

of Time. My phone rang, interrupting my bedroom concert. Glancing at my screen, I couldn't stop the smile that spread across my face.

"Hey," I sang.

"What's up, beautiful? What you up to?"

"Dancing around my room," I chuckled. I plopped on the bed. "What about you?"

"Shit, trying to get up with you. You have plans?"

"No."

"Wanna go out?"

"Where?"

"My sister mentioned some R&B night at this lounge slash restaurant type spot."

"Big bad Ace likes R&B?" I questioned.

"Don't play with me. I'm not gangsta all the time," he chuckled.

"I'm messing with you. What time should I be ready?" I glanced at my cable box and saw it was shortly after five.

"Deanna booked the reservation for seven for me. So I'll be by to grab you around six thirty."

"Okay."

"I won't even hold you because I know you'll need the whole time to get dressed."

"Oh, hush. I'll be ready," I laughed and hung up the phone. I immediately jumped out of bed and headed to my closet to find an outfit. I fingered through my wardrobe and sighed. I grabbed my phone and started a FaceTime call with Jas and Mel.

"It's Saturday, and the center is closed," Jas answered, but Mel didn't.

"Shut up. I need help. Ace is taking me on a date. What do I wear?"

"Where are y'all going?"

"He said some restaurant lounge type of place for an R&B night."

"Oh, that sounds fun. I would do either a cute dress or jeans with a crop top."

"A dress?"

"I gave you another option." I rolled my eyes and continued fingering through my clothes. "I know you have a crop top somewhere in there."

I pulled a pair of distressed jeans from the hanger and tossed them on the bed. I went to my dresser and searched for the crop top turtleneck-type shirt I knew was in there.

"What do I put on my feet?"

"Be comfortable. Throw a pair of retros on or something."

"Oh, I have this blue and white plaid type shirt I can wrap around my waist with my Royal Toe 1s," I suggested.

"Yes! Go ahead and get ready and call me when you're dressed so I can see your outfit."

"Will do." We ended the video call as I headed to the bathroom to turn on the shower. Grabbing my phone, I turned the music back on and placed it on the bathroom sink. Allowing the bathroom to steam up, I grabbed some panties, a bra, and my plush towel before singing as I re-entered the bathroom.

Twenty minutes later, I was climbing out of the shower and started drying off. Just as I was sliding my panties up over my hips, Pandora began playing my favorite song. I dashed into my room to turn on my Bluetooth speaker, so I could play the song louder. I sang along to *Best Friend* by Keyshia Cole as if I were on American Idol. I grabbed my lotion and began lathering it into my skin. Once I was done, I grabbed my jeans and pulled them up. I stood in the full-length mirror and turned side to side to admire how the jeans fit. I was so used to being dressed up for work lately and in leggings on the weekends. I grabbed the shirt and pulled it over my head. I tugged it down a little. I was used to full-length shirts, but Mel had convinced me to buy this damn shirt. I had to admit, it looked really good, but I wasn't used to an exposed midriff. I sighed slightly before heading back into my closet to grab my sneakers.

The music changed, and Monica's *In 3D* came on. Pandora must've been prying on my call because it was definitely getting me ready for tonight. I grabbed my ankle socks and put them on before heading back into the bathroom to style my hair. Twenty-five minutes later, I was completely dressed and back standing in front of the mirror. My low, tight ponytail with slight sideburn calls pulled it all together for me. I smirked as I grabbed my lip gloss off the nightstand. Once I applied it, I blew myself a kiss before grabbing my phone and tapping Jas' name to call her back. As if she was waiting, she answered the phone immediately. I flipped the camera so that she could see the outfit in the mirror.

"Yessss! I love it! It's not over the top, but it's a cute outfit for a lounge-type place. Enjoy yourself, Fin. You deserve it. Let your hair down and forget about all of the problems and work for a night."

"Love you, boo."

"Love you, too, sis. Let me know when you make it back home for the night."

"Will do."

We ended the call again and I started snapping a few pictures in the mirror. I had to admit, I was loving this outfit. Just as I snapped the last picture, Ace was texting me to let me know he was pulling up outside. I started turning the lights in my townhouse off while leaving the light on over my stove. I grabbed my keys, clipped them to my pants, and headed out the door. Just as I made it to the front door, Ace was stepping out of his car. I had to pause because he looked good as fuck!

He wore a pair of blue Robins jeans, with a black Gucci polo shirt, and a crispy pair of black AF1s. He didn't have to get too close to me before his cologne seeped through the air and tickled my nose. I closed my eyes for a second and took a deep breath, sending a silent message to my lady parts down below to calm her hot ass down.

"You good?" he asked.

"Yeah," I smiled, blushing in embarrassment because I was sure he was able to read my thoughts. He flashed his gorgeous smile before he reached out for my hand. I placed my hand in his and he pulled me into his embrace. He felt just as good as he fuckin' smelled. It should be a sin for a man to feel and smell this got damn good. Without realizing it, I was sniffling his neck.

"You wild, Ma," he chuckled.

"You smell really good," I admitted.

"Appreciate it. You do too."

He guided me to the car, opened the door, and closed it once I was in. I leaned over to open his driver's door as much as I could.

"That's some new shit right there," he said as he climbed in.

"What?"

"Niggas usually open the door for a female. Rarely do you hear about a female opening the door for a nigga."

I shrugged. "I'm not your average female."

"I'm learning that."

I settled into the seat as I looked around.

"Clearly this a Jeep Grand Cherokee, but I can tell it's loaded, so it's not a Laredo or a Limited."

"The hell you know about Jeeps, shorty?" he laughed as he pulled away from the curb. "It's a Trackhawk."

"That was my next guess, but I know Overland's are loaded too. Jeeps are one of my favorite SUVs. I rented one before, and the shit was smooth as hell. It's just me, though, so I haven't pushed myself to make the purchase," I admitted.

"It's just me and now Gabby, but I've had my truck since it hit the dealership. It's rare I pull it out, though."

"What year is it?"

"'18."

"If it were me, I would be driving it daily. I love this," I told him as I ran my hand across the door panel.

"Get you one, mama. It won't be just you forever." I didn't say anything and blushed. The remainder of the ride was quiet with just the music playing between us. Shortly after, we pulled up to a small spot on the East Side.

"I've never even been here," I said as I stepped out of the car.

"First of all, next time, wait for me to open the door and let you out. Second of all, it's fairly new."

"Excuse me," I chuckled, throwing my hands in the air. He grabbed my hand and led me inside. Holding the door open, we headed into the dimly lit space. There was soft R&B playing as we stood, waiting for the host.

"Hi. Welcome to Veronica's. Do you have a reservation?" she questioned.

"For two, under Deandre," Ace notified her.

"Great," the host marked something off in front of her before grabbing menus and silverware and advised us to follow her. Ace placed his hand on the small of my back as we followed the hostess to the small table that wasn't too far from the stage. We both sat down, she placed menus in front of us and advised us the wait staff would be over soon. While waiting, I took in the venue.

"This is nice," I said, looking around.

"Yeah, it looks cool."

Before either of us could say anything else, a waitress was back to take our food and drink orders. She recommended a few good dishes and then advised us the band would be on to play within ten minutes. She grabbed the menus and walked off to fill our order. We made small talk until the waitress brought our drinks back just as the band made their way to the stage.

"Heyyyy," the singer sang into the microphone. "How are y'all doing tonight? My name is Sade and I want to welcome you all to Veronica's." The crowd clapped softly. "I'm so glad you all are here. Grab some food, grab some drinks, sit back, and relax as you enjoy the vibes of R&B."

The waitress returned with our drinks and let us know our food would be out shortly. We thanked her and I went back to focusing on the stage. The band began playing the beat of Monica's *Why I Love You So Much*. I immediately started swaying in the seat and closed my eyes as I got lost in Sade's voice. I had to admit, she could sing her ass off and the band matched her perfectly. I snapped my fingers as I sang the song softly. I couldn't stop the smile that graced my face.

Out of the corner of my eye, I could see Ace staring at me with a slight smile on his face. I immediately stopped and couldn't help but blush and drop my head.

"Nah, don't stop. I love what I see."

I placed both of my hands over my face and tried to stop smiling, but I couldn't. Ace was making me feel things that I hadn't felt in so long and I would be lying if I said I wanted it to stop. The waitress saved me by placing the food in front of us. I couldn't lie, my stomach growled at the scent of the Bourbon Street Chicken, topped with seared shrimp, garlic mashed potatoes, and broccoli and cheese. Looking at Ace's plate, he simply had a fried seafood platter, and I would be lying if I said I wasn't tempted to dig my hands in his plate.

"Don't tell me you're one of those," he chuckled just as the band switched songs.

"One of what?"

"One of those who order their own food, yet don't want it and would prefer to eat mine."

"Oh no, I'm gonna eat mine, but I may or may not pick at yours too," I shrugged as if it was nothing as I ate a scoop of mashed potatoes. He laughed, shook his head, and began covering his seafood in hot sauce. We made small talk while enjoying the music and a few drinks. Once we were done eating, the waitress offered us dessert, but I was too full for anything else. We remained at the table as the music played, and I was definitely enjoying myself. The sounds of R&B were always relaxing to me, and I was always able to get lost in the moment.

"You want to dance?" Ace asked me, surprising me at the same time.

"You dance?"

He stood up and walked around the table to grab my hand.

"There's a lot about me that you have yet to learn. However, if you stick around long enough, you'll find out just who Deandre really is." I smiled as I stood from the seat and followed him to the small dance area, just as the band switched and Xscape's, *Do You Want To*, began playing. Ace dropped his hands to my lower back, and I wrapped my arms around his neck. I looked into his eyes as we two stepped to the music. I tried hard but failed at not smiling. "What does your young ass know about this?"

"Don't play with me. I love me some 90s R&B," I responded, cocking my head to the side. We slow danced to a few more songs. I rested my head on his chest, and he placed his chin on my head as we swayed together. One thing was for sure, I was glad I wore sneakers rather than heels. I opened my eyes when I felt Ace plant soft kisses on my forehead. I smiled and melted like putty, squeezing him tighter.

Looking up at him, our eyes locked for a short period before Ace leaned down and smashed his lips into mine. His lips were softer than I could have imagined. At that moment, it didn't even matter that we were standing in the middle of a lounge. To me, there was nobody standing there except for me and him. I could hear SWV's, *Weak,* begin to play. We broke the kiss, and I laid my head back on his chest. I could relate as I danced wrapped in Ace's arms, I felt weaker than I had felt in a long time.

I didn't want to jump to conclusions about where Ace and I were going, but wherever this ride was going to take us, I was ready to be in the front seat and ready to go.

Chapter Ten

Deandre 'Ace' Lemetti

Four Months Later…

"Dre, I got your shirt," Deanna yelled.

"What damn shirt?" I asked. I was frustrated with this whole day, and it was hardly even noon. Today was Gabby's first birthday and I had blown more than a fuckin' bag on it. I couldn't believe that my baby girl was one. This fuckin' year flew by. It had been damn near a year since she was literally left on my doorstep, but it has been the most complicated, yet loving year of my life.

"The family shirts that I had done for the party."

"Why are you so damn extra, Deanna?"

"Shut up and put the damn shirt on." She tossed the shirt on my bed. I sighed and went into my closet to pull out a pair of jeans. My phone vibrated in the pocket of my basketball shorts.

Pulling it out, I saw it was Infinity.

"What's up, beautiful?" I answered. Infinity and I had been kicking it for the last few months. We weren't official or fuckin', we were just kicking it as strictly friends. I couldn't lie. She was definitely someone I could see myself with, but I wasn't about to push it.

"Hey, what time does the party start?"

"Shit I have no idea, to be honest. My mother and sister have been handling all that shit."

She chuckled. "Can you find out and let me know?"

"I got you."

"Thank you."

She hung up and I went to find my sister. I found her fighting with Gabby to get dressed. Every time she tried to put Gabby's shirt over her head, Gabby pulled and moved her head. The view was actually funny.

"What time does this party start?"

"Two."

"A'ight."

I shot Infinity a text letting her know what time the party started. I went back into my room to roll myself a blunt. I felt like this party was going to stress me the fuck out. I had no idea who Deanna invited, but something in me was telling me it was going to be some bullshit. I was gonna try my best to actually enjoy it because my baby girl only turned one once.

"Dre, we're leaving in an hour," my sister yelled.

"A'ight."

That gave me more than enough time to smoke and relax for a little bit.

Two hours later, I was walking into the party. I knew Deanna was going to talk shit, but one of my little niggas called saying he was out of work, and I had to bring him what he needed. It was what it was, but she would be a'ight.

Walking into the party, it was in full swing. Deanna had it decorated in a Boss Baby theme, and it was decked the fuck out. She definitely took the statement spare no expense to the next level. For crying out loud, she had one of them people show up in a Boss Baby costume. I shook my head and chuckled but didn't say anything. I greeted a few family members and scooped up Gabby off the floor, smothering her with kisses. Her giggles melted a nigga's heart for real.

Infinity walked up and interrupted me and Gabby's moment. I didn't mind, and neither did Gabby because the moment she saw her, her face lit up and she immediately reached for her. Infinity grabbed her from my arms and began planting kisses all over her face.

"Happy birthday, beautiful," she said, kissing her again. Gabby kissed her back before squirming to get down. Infinity placed her on the floor and Gabby took off. "Hey, you," she smiled as she leaned in and gave me a hug.

"Thanks for coming," I told her as I planted a kiss on her forehead. She handed me the gift bag and we walked over to the table that was loaded with gifts for Gabby.

"Of course! I wouldn't miss her birthday for anything. You know Gabby is my baby," she smiled.

"I don't know who she likes more; me or you," I joked with her.

"Stop! You know I can't replace the love she has for you," she laughed. Infinity and I walked over to the bar and grabbed a drink, before sitting at one of the tables to talk. I watched as Gabby ran around her party, and I knew she was going to run herself right to sleep, which I was fine with. The harder she played, the faster she would go to sleep. I glanced at the door, and it was as if nothing else around me was happening. I just knew my eyes were playing tricks on me. I blinked a few times to see if the view would change, but it didn't. She looked timid walking in and started looking around. When her eyes landed on me, she had a soft smile on her face. At the same time, Gabby ran into Infinity's arms, and she picked her up. Aaliyah's eyes lit up at the site of Gabby, but her smile dropped when I stood in between her and Gabby's view.

I marched in her direction and the look of fear filled her face. I grabbed her arm roughly and pulled her toward the exit. The moment we were outside, I damn near pushed her into the brick wall.

"What the fuck are you doing here?" I snapped.

"I-I came to celebrate my daughter's birthday," she stuttered.

"Do not piss me off, Aaliyah. You dropped her off on my

porch a damn year ago, you didn't bother to fuckin' check up on her, and now you just waltz back in like all is well? You can play with yourself, but you won't play with my daughter," I told her.

"She's my daughter too, Deandre. You cannot keep me from her."

I laughed in her face. Probably harder than she thought I would.

"Bitch, she ain't shit to you. Remember when you weren't ready to give up your party life to be a mother? Keep that same energy. She's been amazing without you. She doesn't need you. The only way you'll see her is if a judge forces me to give her to you. Other than that, go back to acting like she doesn't exist."

I turned and walked back inside the hall where we were having the party. I couldn't lie, I was over this shit and wanted to shut it down, but the sight of Gabby made me realize it wasn't about me. I plopped into the seat next to Infinity who was finishing off her Shirley Temple.

"Is everything okay?" she asked.

"Shit, it was until that shit happened," I said shaking my head.

"Care to talk about it?"

I noticed this dumb bitch made her way back inside the hall again and was looking around. It was taking everything in me to not get up and literally drag her from this place. Infinity must've followed my eyes to where Aaliyah was standing.

"Who is she?" she asked.

"Gabby's incubator," I responded between gritted teeth. "I don't know why she's here, but the view of her is just setting me the fuck off. Bitch left my daughter on my fuckin' stoop and here it is her first birthday, and she wanna pop the fuck back up."

"Remember, it's about Gabby," she said grabbing my arm.

"Gabby doesn't know her. Gabby doesn't need her. I don't even know why the fuck she reappeared."

I was clenching my jaw so hard, that I was surprised I wasn't cracking my own damn teeth. Deanna came and stood in front of me with her hand on her hip.

"Why are you over here looking all pissy in the face?" she questioned.

"Tryna figure out why the fuck Aaliyah is here."

"I invited her," she said nonchalantly.

"You did what?" I shouted louder than I anticipated. "Tell me you're fuckin' lying, Deanna."

"What the hell is the problem? That's Gabby's mother."

"Deanna, I'll slap the shit out of you. Are you fuckin' kidding me right now?"

"What? She messaged me asking about Gabby and I thought it would be fine to tell her to come see her daughter for her birthday." If this were a cartoon, the smoke would be barreling out of my ears. I wanted to show my ass in this place, but I knew it wouldn't end well.

"You're not her fuckin' parent, Deanna. That's not a call that you have the right to make."

"Are you serious right now, Deandre? As much as I do for that little girl, that's what you're gonna say to me?" I could see her feelings were hurt, but at this point, it was fuck her feelings.

"You do for her as her fuckin' aunt. You don't make calls on when this stupid ass bitch can walk in and out of my daughter's fuckin' life. Knowing what the fuck she did, you should have never even tried to allow this shit. You should have told me when this bitch reached out to you. I don't know why the fuck you would ever think this shit is okay. Fuck her, fuck this party, and at this point, fuck you." I turned around, grabbed Gabby from Infinity, and walked out of the hall. I couldn't believe the shit Deanna pulled and it would be a long time before I would ever trust her again. If anybody knew, Deanna knew how I felt about Aaliyah with this situation. The fact that she would go behind my back and do this made me feel a type of way about her, and one thing I never wanted to do was be on the outs with my sister. However, if she should have anyone's back, it should be mine. Yet, in this case, Deanna chose the opp. There wasn't much that could hurt me, but that shit hurt me deeply.

Chapter Eleven

Deanna Lemetti

I stood stuck in place as tears filled my eyes. The look I saw on Deandre's face is one that I've never seen, and for once, I feel like I truly overstepped my boundary and, in the process, damn near killed my brother. The entire party froze and was staring in my direction as I looked at the door that Dre had just walked out of with Gabby.

"Deanna, what the hell happened?" my mother asked me as she walked up to me. Aaliyah stood in the same spot by the door looking around. "What is she doing here?" My mother followed my view and spotted Aaliyah.

"I-I thought it would be a good idea for her to come to celebrate the baby's birthday, and Deandre just flipped," I explained as I wiped my face.

"Oh, no," my mother sighed. "This was not the place for that. I get what you were trying to do, but this wasn't the time.

Especially without talking to him about it. You know Gabby is a soft spot for him. Oh, lord." My mother gripped her forehead and dropped her head back. She sighed before walking away. My mother walked up to Aaliyah and pulled her off to the side. I noticed Dre's friend who had been helping with Gabby was still sitting there and looking uncomfortable. I walked off to the bathroom to try and get myself together. I pulled out my phone and dialed Dre's number. The phone barely rang twice before he pushed my call over to voicemail. I sighed as I called a few more times before giving up. I figured I would go out and start cleaning up the party.

Walking out of the bathroom, the hall was extremely quiet, and everyone was lending a hand with breaking down the party stuff. Dre's friend walked over to me by the gift table.

"Hey, is there anything I can help with?" she questioned. I looked her up and down. I had to admit, she was pretty as hell.

"You're Infinity, right? You own the daycare?" I nodded. "I thought so. I'm sorry you had to witness this. I promise this is not how we normally are."

"Oh no, you're fine. Every family has its issues, including mine. There's no judgment," she smiled. "I wish I could have met you under better circumstances, but it's nice to meet you outside of the center. I've heard a lot about you and your mom too."

"Hopefully, it's all good things," I smiled.

"It was. All he talked about was how much he loves you and

your mom, and how much you guys help him with Gabby."

"Yeah, and right now he hates my guts," I admitted, with my eyes filling with tears again.

"Oh, no. I highly doubt he hates you. One thing I did see on his face was hurt, but he cannot and does not hate you. I'm not sure exactly what happened, but I know the look of hurt all too well. I will say just give it time. You know your brother better than I do though," she shrugged.

"I appreciate it." Infinity dove right in helping with stripping the tables and chairs. We bagged up the décor, popped all the balloons, swept the floor, and wiped down the tables. An hour and a half later, we were loading up my mother's car with the décor to return to the decorator, and I put the gifts into my car to give myself a reason to go to Dre's house.

I waved to Infinity and gave my mom a kiss on the cheek before heading toward Dre's. I tried calling him again, but he still was pushing my calls to voicemail. It took me less than twenty minutes to get to his house. His car was in the driveway, so I knew he was just ignoring me to be an asshole. I sighed as I grabbed a few gift bags and headed toward the door. I used my key to let myself in and found him lounging on the couch with Gabby sleeping on his chest. My brother looked like he had the weight of the world on his shoulders, making me feel worse than what I already felt.

"What, Deanna?" he blurted out without even opening his eyes.

"How did you know it was me?" I asked, setting the gifts on the floor, and closing the door behind me.

"Because I knew once I didn't answer the phone, you were coming here. What do you want?"

I sighed and walked over to the couch to sit next to him.

"I'm sorry, Dre. I didn't think you would be upset. I honestly thought you would be happy with the fact she decided to be there," I shrugged.

"Deanna, really?" he looked at me like I was speaking a totally different language. "When have you ever heard me say I wanted Aaliyah around? She's missed so much that Gabby doesn't even recognize her. I wish she would have been there since day one, but she chose the streets over her kid. That's not some shit I could ever or would ever forget. My daughter didn't ask to be here, and her mother just dropped her off on the porch like she was yesterday's fuckin' trash. Tell me Gabby deserved that shit, Deanna. Go ahead and I'll call Aaliyah right now and allow her back into Gabby's life with no issue," he snapped. I knew everything he said was right. Gabby didn't deserve that shit. I sucked in a deep breath and wiped the rapidly falling tears that were cascading down my face.

"I'm sorry, Dre. I just... I thought it would be what's best for Gabby. Everyone deserves their mother just as much as they deserve their father. I figured with us not having dad around, that you would want Aaliyah to be around whenever she got her mind right," I admitted. As I said the shit out loud, I realized how dumb it sounded.

"The difference is Dad *couldn't* be there because he's dead! Aaliyah chose not to be there because she didn't want to stop partying. I didn't ask shit of Aaliyah but to give this shit a chance. She decided it wasn't for her. Fine, but that doesn't mean she gets to pick and choose when she can come back. She's not about to drop in and out of my daughter's life like she's a toy. That shit isn't fair to anybody."

"I know. I realize that now. I'm sorry. I really am. I thought I was doing something right that would benefit Gabby, but I didn't think about how you would feel about it. I fucked up."

The room became silent between us. I wanted Dre to say something, but I knew he was in his feelings and after hearing his explanation, I didn't blame him. I leaned over and placed a kiss on his cheek and then Gabby's cheek before standing to head out the door.

"I love you, Deanna. I'll always love you. I know you love Gabby and will never do anything to hurt her. However, when it comes to Aaliyah, please let me be the one to make the decisions." I nodded and walked towards his front door. "Let me know when you make it home."

"I have a few more of her gifts in the car."

"A'ight. Give me a second and I'll come grab them."

He stood and walked toward Gabby's room. I sighed and wiped my face. I hated it when my brother was mad at me. Growing up, he truly was my best friend, so for him to be mad at me did something to me. Within a few minutes, he was back and following me outside to grab the remaining gifts. He planted a kiss on my forehead and watched me pull off to head home. I loved my niece and that went without saying, but this would be the first and last time I ever got involved with her parents again in life.

Chapter Twelve

Aaliyah Murphy

I drove around aimlessly after leaving the hall where Ace had Gabby's party. I had to admit, the shit looked amazing. When my eyes landed on my baby girl, I couldn't believe how big she had gotten. I wasn't expecting Ace to react to me the way he had. I mean I expected him to be upset, but I figured with my reappearance he would be happy to see since he wanted this family so bad. I was sadly mistaken because the anger in his eye was something I had never seen before.

The last year for me had been wild. It's uncommon for mothers to not want to be a mother, but truthfully, I didn't want to have a baby. I expressed how much I didn't want children to Ace, but he begged me. I mean literally begged me. I figured going through the pregnancy would allow me to change my mind. Unfortunately, it didn't. When I had my daughter, I thought it would be fun just watching her grow and doing mother-daughter shit, but it wasn't that. I no longer could up and leave when I wanted to. The days of partying with my girlfriends were over. She required a lot of attention, and at twenty-two, it wasn't something I was ready to give.

I had stopped communicating with Ace during my pregnancy because he was becoming overbearing. What some would consider a caring father to be, I found to be annoying. He was constantly asking me if I ate, how I was feeling, or if I needed anything, and I honestly just wanted it to stop. It probably sounds dumb, but clearly, I was in my feelings trying to accept the changes I was going through. Looking back at it now, I regret it because, during our entire situationship, he had been nothing but loving and caring toward me.

After a few weeks of trying to parent the baby by myself, I was done. I felt like I couldn't do enough, and I was tired. I wrote a note, packed her bag, stuffed her incomplete birth certificate in the diaper bag, and headed to drop her off to someone who wanted her because, at the time, I didn't. I wasn't ready to give up my early adult years, and since Ace wanted her so bad, he could have her. After I dropped her off, I called up my girls and told them I was free. The first few nights of partying were cool until they started asking me where the baby was. When I told them the truth, they slowly pulled themselves from me. I found myself reaching out to them and not getting any sort of response. It wasn't until I ran into my home girl Amanda in the store that she told me she couldn't fuck with someone who gave their child up for a life of partying. I tried to explain my reasoning, but she wasn't tryna hear it. After losing my friends, I worked part-time jobs trying to support myself while still trying to have a life. It didn't take long for me to realize how bad I had fucked up. I knew I couldn't go back to Ace while not having my shit together, so I enrolled in classes to get my medical assistant certificate and landed a full-time job. I had just moved into a one-bedroom townhouse and purchased a cheap car. I couldn't financially give my daughter the life that Ace could, but this time, I wanted to try. I tried to find Ace on social media, but I couldn't find his page. I was easily able to find his sister and was surprised when she accepted my request. I was able to see a few pictures of my daughter and learned Ace had named her Gabrielle. She was beautiful and looked just like Ace. Just as I suspected, he was taking very good care of her.

It took me a while before I was able to reach out to Deanna. I held my breath when I saw she had read my message. I just knew that she was going to hate me like I was sure Ace did. She gave me hope when she invited me to Gabby's party. It would be the first time I laid eyes on my daughter in almost a year and the first time I would see Ace in over a year.

An hour later, I pulled up to my townhouse. Just as I was climbing out, my phone alerted me of a Facebook message. My heart skipped a beat when I saw that it was a message from Deanna.

Dee Lemetti: *I'm sorry. I never expected that to happen, but I* *also wasn't thinking about how Deandre would feel. I should have spoken to him before giving you the okay to come. I'm sure that's not how you expected to reunite with your daughter. I'll just say give him time to see if he wants to allow you back in her life.*

I scrunched up my face, and my fingers immediately started responding.

Me: *Allow me in her life? I'm her mother! I have just as many rights to her as he does.*

I would be lying if I said Deanna's message didn't piss me off. I wasn't the ideal mother, but nonetheless, I was still her mother. I didn't like the fact that one person could decide whether I saw her again or not. My phone vibrated once more.

Dee Lemetti: *Do you remember that you left her on his porch? He has gone through all of the legal aspects and now has sole custody of her. He does not have to let you do anything. Your best bet is to try and work with him rather than go against him. He would die before he let anyone take her from him. Either play by his rules or just stay away from him. That's the only warning I can give.*

I didn't even bother to respond. I walked into my townhouse and plopped on the couch. I wanted to be involved in my daughter's life. I had finally started to get myself together to be there for her, and now it seems to have all been for nothing.

One thing was for sure, I wanted to be involved in my daughter's life, and I would spend whatever it cost to get those rights whether Ace liked it or not.

Chapter Thirteen

Infinity Morrison

I pulled into my driveway thirty minutes after leaving the hall. I sighed as I killed the engine and just as I was stepping out, my phone rang. I was surprised to see it was Ace.

"Hey," I answered before the voicemail could pick up.

"Are you busy?"

"No, I just got home," I let him know, activating the alarm.

"Can you swing through? I just…" he paused, and the phone got silent. "I need to talk to someone."

"Okay. I'll be there. Do you need me to bring anything?"

"Nah. I just need your listening ear and a voice of reason. I just sent you the address."

"Okay. I'm on my way." We disconnected the call, and I hopped back in the car headed toward his house. A million and one thoughts were running through my mind. The whole ride to Ace's house, I replayed the scene of the party in my head. I still couldn't believe Gabby's mother popped up like all was well and was even more surprised for his sister to say that she invited her. One thing I could say for sure was she hurt her brother with what she did, but I knew he would forgive her eventually.

It took me less than twenty minutes to reach his house, and I had to admit, it was a beautiful place. I pulled into his driveway next to his car and shot him a text letting him know that I was outside. He quickly responded that the door was unlocked. I grabbed my keys and purse before locking my car and heading inside. He sat on the couch with the side table light on, his feet kicked up on the table, and a blunt lit. I locked the door behind me and slowly made my way into the kitchen. He had the TV on, but his focus wasn't on what was playing.

"Are you okay?" I asked taking a seat. He sighed before taking a long pull of his blunt and holding in the smoke. He blew it out, ashed his blunt, and then closed his eyes.

"Am I doing the right thing?"

"Regarding what?"

"Keeping Gabby from her mom."

I sighed. I instantly thought back to my situation with my son and Jermaine.

"Follow your heart. I know you want nothing more than to protect your daughter. As long as you're doing what's best for her, then you are always doing the right thing."

"But every child needs their mother," he voiced and took another pull from his blunt.

"And every child deserves honest and genuine love. They deserve to have their hearts protected. Her mother has already left her once, who's to say she won't do it again? I can't tell you what to do because I'm a firm believer in doing what needs to be done to protect your child. Me, because of the emotional trauma inflicted on me by my ex, I never intended to let him know about my son. I never wanted my son to experience any of that, so I planned on doing what I felt was right. You've done a helluva job with her during this time. You have an amazing support system. Right now, she's not looking for her. She probably doesn't even know what a mom is, but when she gets older, she might have questions."

"How would I tell her that her mother left her on my porch?" he questioned.

"Honestly, I don't know, but it'll be a very long time before you have to cross that bridge. Right now, you just keep being the best father that you can be to her. She deserves that. Never let anyone try and take that from you. Take everything day by day and the right answer on what you should do will come to you."

The living room became silent between the two of us. He continued smoking before he sat up and rubbed his hands together.

"Are you busy tonight?"

"No, I'm here." I offered him a small smile.

"Can you keep an eye on Gabby for me? I just gotta run out for a few."

"That's fine."

"She's up in her bedroom. You can either sleep in the guest room or take my room and I'll sleep in the guest room. Whichever you want to do is fine."

"Okay."

"I'll show you to her room."

We both stood and I followed him up the stairs. He pointed to the guest room and then peeked in Gabby's room at her. He then opened the door to his room, and for a moment, I got stuck. His bed was unmade, but it was huge and looked comfortable as fuck. I could only imagine sinking into his mattress and getting some of the best sleep of my life.

"If you want something to sleep in, I have some basketball shorts and t-shirts in the dresser right there," he pointed out as he walked into his closet. He was in there for a few minutes before he came out dressed in an all-black Champion sweatsuit with a pair of crisp black Air Force Ones. "Do you need anything before I dip?"

"No, I think I'm good."

"If you get hungry, there's some shit in the fridge and freezer, or you can order something."

"Got it."

"I'll be back shortly." I nodded as I watched him lick his lips and walk out the bedroom door. I closed my eyes, inhaled, and squeezed my thighs tightly together. That man was fine as fuck and seeing him in his thugged out attire had me wanting to do some damn things to his ass! I opened my eyes and went through his drawers until I found a pair of boxers and a T-shirt. I decided to take a quick shower and get some rest. I wasn't sure if Gabby was still one who woke up in the middle of the night or not.

Within twenty-five minutes, I was out of the shower and putting my clothes in the corner of his room. I made a mental note to throw them in a bag in the morning. I sat on his bed before I heard Gabby whining through the small baby monitor on his nightstand. I headed to her room and found her stirring in her bed. When she spotted me, she offered me a smile. Picking her up, she instantly put her head on my shoulder. It was literally seconds before I could hear her slight snore. Rather than put her back in her crib, I sat down on Ace's bed and laid Gabby down in the middle. Just as I suspected, his mattress felt like a damn cloud. I knew it wasn't going to be long before I passed out.

Looking at the cable box, I saw it was shortly after ten, however, I felt like I had been running around all day. I laid down and browsed the channels before settling on *Chopped*. It wasn't long before I was dozing off.

Chapter Fourteen

Deandre 'Ace' Lemetti

"A'ight, I'm out," I told my nigga, Los. I dapped him up as I stood from the VIP couch. I had stopped by Los' earlier to chop it up with him, and his ass had convinced me to come down to Club Encore for a few drinks. The vibe was dope and what I needed to get my mind off my personal life. My street business was taking the fuck off, yet it seemed my personal life was in shambles. I walked around the small circle and dapped up the rest of the crew that popped out with us. It was shortly after one in the morning. I wasn't drunk but between the blunts and bottles, I was feeling nice as hell.

The valet pulled my Benz up. I tipped him, hopped in, and took off. The breeze from the late-night air felt good as hell. My stomach growled, so I decided to stop at Wendy's and grab me something quick. I tried to call Infinity, but when she didn't answer, I figured she was asleep. I ordered my food and headed home, stuffing my face on the way.

I shoved the last of my burger into my mouth just as I pulled up to the crib. All of the lights in the house were out, so my suspicions of Infinity being asleep were confirmed. As quietly as I could, I let myself into the house and threw my trash away. I headed upstairs and peeked into the guest room, but I saw it was empty. Peeking into Gabby's room, I saw her bed was empty too. My heart rate sped up for a second because I knew the couch was empty, as well as the two bedrooms. I didn't realize I had been holding my breath until I opened my bedroom door and spotted Infinity and Gabby passed out. I couldn't help the smile that graced my face. Taking out my phone, I had to take a picture of the scene before me. I went into my closet to strip down and take a quick shower to wash the club scent off of me.

Part of me wanted to climb into the bed with Gabby and Infinity, but I didn't know how she would feel about waking up beside me. So after my shower, I headed into the guest bedroom. I didn't realize how tired I was until I was woken up the following morning by the scent of breakfast. I still had the remote control in my hand and realized I never even changed the channel. I stretched before climbing out of bed and headed to handle my hygiene. I peeked back into my bedroom and noticed the bed was made and both Infinity and Gabby weren't there. I allowed my nose to lead me to the kitchen where Gabby was sitting in her highchair, stuffing her face with a cut-up pancake. She looked at me and gave me a huge smile, showing off the four little teeth she had.

"Good morning," I called out so that she wouldn't jump when she turned around.

"Hey."

"I could get used to this," I told her, leaning across the island counter.

"What you mean?"

"Waking up and finding you in my kitchen. Shit's sexy if I must admit," I told her. I watched as she tried to force herself not to blush. I looked her up and down as she walked around the kitchen in my clothes. "Be my girl," I stated, breaking the silence. I surprised myself with it, but I would be lying if I said I hadn't been thinking about it for a while.

"Huh?"

"Stop acting like you ain't hear me," I chuckled.

"How do you know you want me to be your girl?" She leaned against the counter behind her and gave me her undivided attention.

"Watching the way that you love my daughter means the world to me. Whenever I need you, you're there for me, even if it's just to talk. Over the last few months of us talking, I've learned a lot about you. Despite all that you've been through, you never gave up, and I admire the fuck out of that." She blushed and dropped her head. She then cut her eyes at me with a sneaky smile.

"Let me ask you a few questions to see how much you pay

attention, Mr. Lemetti."

"Go ahead."

"What's my favorite color?"

I laughed and dropped my head. She was definitely testing a nigga because this was something we discussed during one of our first conversations. Little did she know, I paid attention and memorized shit that most wouldn't think twice about.

"You have more than one. Pink and blue." Her eyes bucked a little bit.

"What's my middle name?"

"Janae."

"How long have I worked with children?"

"Since you were sixteen. Your favorite fast-food spot is Chipotle. Jasmine and Melanie are your best friends. Your dream car is a Range Rover. Your birthday is April 12th. You enjoy reading and relaxing after a long day of work. Fruity drinks are your thing. Anything else?"

She slowly nodded her head and did a slow clap.

"I'm impressed."

"Don't be. I'm not your typical nigga, love. When I'm interested in something, or in this case, someone, I listen to store the important details. When I'm in a relationship, I'm dedicated to keeping you happy so that you don't have to look elsewhere."

"Okay."

"Okay? That's your answer?" I questioned. She busted out laughing.

"I mean you didn't really ask. You kind of just threw it out there as a suggestion type of thing," she laughed.

I cocked my head to the side. "Infinity, will you be my girlfriend?"

"Yes," she blushed. I walked around the counter and stood directly in front of her. I stood at least seven inches taller than her, so I had to bend down a little to plant a kiss on her lips. I slipped my tongue into her mouth, and she sucked on it gently. I felt my dick bricking up, but I knew she wasn't trying to take it there just yet. I heard Gabby giggling and broke the kiss. I stared into Infinity's eyes as is stepped back.

"Lips just as soft as I remembered," he told her. She blushed and dropped her head. "What did you cook?"

"Pancakes, cheese eggs, maple sausage, bacon, and the toast is in the toaster."

"Damn. Too bad I don't eat any of that," I told her. I watched as she paused and dropped the spatula on the counter.

"Are you serious?" she questioned.

"I'm just fuckin' with you," I laughed. "I haven't had a home-cooked breakfast meal in a long ass time."

"Jackass."

I watched as Gabby sat back and grabbed her cup of juice. Staring at her, I couldn't help but think that all Aaliyah had missed out on. My mind then began to wander on whether I wanted to give her a chance. A part of me felt like she could be a helluva mother, yet another part of me couldn't get over how she left Gabby the way she did.

Infinity placing my plate in front of me broke me from my trance.

"Stop overthinking. Like I told you, it'll all work out." She winked before turning around to make her own place. She was right. I wouldn't figure this out this fast, and it was best for me to just let it play out the way it was supposed to. Infinity came back with her plate, placed it down, and then went back for the juice. I watched as she closed her eyes, said a silent prayer, and then dug in.

"So you just ain't gonna pray with me?" I questioned, grabbing a piece of bacon.

"I wasn't sure if it was your thing, however, I did pray for you."

I nodded and dug into my plate. I had to admit, the shit was bomb as fuck.

"This is real good. I appreciate it." We made small talk as we continued our meal, and when we were done, Infinity grabbed the dishes and placed them in the sink. "What are your plans for today?" I asked her.

"I usually use Sundays to get ready for the work week."

"What does that entail?" I asked her, placing Gabby on the counter as I used baby wipes to clean her hands and face.

"Laundry, ironing, food shopping, things like that. Why what's up?"

"Just asking."

"What about you?"

I shrugged. "I gotta run and check on a few things. I'll probably see if Gabby can hang with my moms for a little while."

"Oh okay. I'm about to head home though."

"Leaving us already?" I fake pouted, as I softly patted Gabby's back.

"Don't start," she chuckled. "Call me if you need me." She walked over and planted a kiss on Gabby's cheek as she started dozing off, and then a juicy, wet kiss on my lips.

"Keep doing that and you won't make it out the door," I told her.

"Whatever," she laughed. I watched as she headed toward my room, I'm assuming to grab her clothes. Within ten minutes, she was heading to the door in my clothes and with her clothes in her hand. "I'll see you later."

"A'ight, mama. Let me know when you make it home."

"I will." I followed her out to her car to make sure she was safe before planting another kiss on her lips and watching her pull off.

It had been a long ass time since I had done the relationship shit, but truthfully, Infinity made me want to give that shit a chance. I had been feeling her for a while but watching her with Gabby solidified that we couldn't let her go.

Chapter Fifteen

Infinity Morrison

A s soon as I turned off Ace's street, I called Jas and Mel on FaceTime. I pulled into Dunkin' to order a coffee just as they answered.

"Hey, hoe," Jas answered.

"What the hell you want?" Mel chimed in before I could even respond.

"Y'all!" I shrieked. "Hold on. Let me order my coffee before I tell y'all."

"Oh boy. Let me sit up for this because I know you're about to tell us some wild shit," Jas laughed. I ordered my coffee and pulled off toward my house.

"So, y'all know how I have been helping with Gabby, right? Well, her dad and I have also been talking for a few months," I explained.

"I knew it, bitch! That man is fine as fuck, so I probably

would have done the same thing. I'm not even gonna lie," Mel said. We all laughed as I continued.

"Anyway, yesterday was her birthday, so I went to her birthday party. It was honestly cute as hell. Gabby was having a blast. All of a sudden, Ace's entire demeanor changed. It was almost as if he morphed into an entirely different person. He storms off, snatches this lady up, and then walks outside. I seemed to be the only one who noticed, so I sat there waiting for him to come back. Turns out, Gabby's mother reappeared."

"Where the hell has she been?" Jas asked.

"When Gabby was an infant, apparently, she left Gabby on his porch with a note, baby items, and a blank birth certificate form. Ace has been raising her with the help of his mother and sister ever since. The next thing I know, he comes back inside, sits down, and is trying to calm down. His sister walks up to him and ultimately tells him that the mother had reached out to her, and she thought it would be okay to invite her to the damn party."

"Wait what?"

"Girl! Told the chick to come to the damn party after she missed a whole damn year of her child's life. I have never seen someone flip so damn quick. I'm sure if he was a female, or his sister was a nigga, he definitely would have laid hands on her. He snatched Gabby up and left in the middle of the damn party. I'm not gonna lie, it was awkward as fuck sitting there because he and Gabby were the only two there that I actually knew. I mean I've met his mom and sister at the center, but I don't know them outside of that. I helped them straighten up before I left. Then, as I got home, he called me and asked me to come by."

"Y'all fucked?" Mel asked.

"No bitch." I couldn't help but laugh.

"Shit, you should have," Jas chimed in.

I rolled my eyes and shook my head.

"Y'all bitches always want a bitch to jump on a dick."

"Hell yeah," they shouted in unison.

"Anyway, what happened after that?" Jas questioned.

"I went by, and we talked. He asked me my opinion on the situation with Gabby's mom and what I would do in that situation. He asked if I felt he was wrong. We just vibed, honestly. Then he asked me to sit with Gabby while he ran out. I ended up falling asleep, woke up, and made him breakfast this morning before I left. He asked me to be his girlfriend."

"I hope your ass said yes," Mel chimed in.

I smiled hard like a teenager. "I did."

"Good! I'm happy for you, boo. I wish you could see your face when you talk about him and Gabby. I haven't seen your face light up like this in a while, so I can tell he makes you happy. Just let him know that we don't play about you. If he tries to play you, I have no issue busting a cap in his big ass. At least I'll try," Jas said, serious as a heart attack with Mel nodding in agreement.

"Y'all are wild, but I love y'all. I just pulled into my

driveway. Let me get in here and start my Sunday routine. I'll talk to you bitches later."

"Love you," they said simultaneously.

"Love y'all too."

We ended the call just as I killed the engine. I shot Ace a text letting him know that I was home before heading inside. I kicked my shoes off and then headed to gather my laundry so I could start washing clothes. I turned on my Bluetooth speaker and began moving about the house as I started the first load of laundry, pulled something out of the freezer for dinner, and put away my dishes. In the midst of my Sunday clean-up, I heard my phone go off. Grabbing my phone from the counter, I noticed a Facebook message come through. My heart started racing when I saw the name.

Maine Attraction.

I swallowed hard as I tapped on the name and scrolled the profile. Jermaine had found me, and I didn't know how I felt. It had been years since I had even seen him, let alone spoken to him. All the emotions of our relationship flooded back, and I shuttered. I went back to my inbox to read the message.

Wow! You spoke so much about opening a daycare and you finally did it. I'm proud of you, love. Hope all is well and maybe we can catch up and hang out.

I rolled my eyes hard as hell. I couldn't believe after all we had been through that he would think I would want to catch up. The last four years had been peaceful without Jermaine. I healed a lot from the trauma he caused and the passing of my son. I refused to go backward.

Thanks, but no thanks. I would rather not.

I hit send, took a screenshot, and sent it to Jas and Mel. I locked the phone and set it back down before going back to what I was doing. At least I tried. It was hard because I still couldn't get over the fact that Jermaine had even reached out to me. I went into my room, grabbed my son's urn, and sat on the bed. Staring at it, I couldn't stop the tears that welled in my eyes. I missed my son. I cried for the fear of never being able to have children. I cried a lot when I first split from Jermaine and lost my son, but this cry felt different. I felt as if a weight was being lifted from my shoulders. I didn't even know what the weight was from.

Then it hit me. For so long, Jermaine found ways to demean me. When I was with Jermaine, I never felt like he supported anything I wanted to do. He never encouraged me to do anything. Anytime I talked about something I wanted to do; Jermaine brushed it off as if the shit I was saying was far-fetched. When I left, I felt like I was failing my unborn. I cried a lot and often for what my child wouldn't have. With a lot of soul-searching and counseling, I was able to remind myself of what I could do. Even after I lost my son, I felt myself falling into the space of doubt again, but I pushed through and made promises to my son that I would have that center in his memory. I also felt like I had to prove to Jermaine that I could do the shit he never supported me with. To read his message and to simply see him say he was proud, did something to me.

I bonded with my son for a good ten minutes before kissing his urn and placing it back in its rightful spot. I headed back toward the laundry closet to swap the laundry and then to the kitchen to start on dinner. Just as I was about to dump the meat into a bowl to season, my phone rang. Scooping it up, I saw it was a FaceTime from Ace.

"Hey," I smiled.

"What's up, mama? What you doing?"

"I was just about to get started on dinner. What about you?"

"Shit, I'm about to drop Gabby off at my mom's before heading out. What you cooking?"

"I'm putting some steak tips in the crockpot to make Mongolian beef over rice."

"Gabby and I are coming by for dinner. Do you need me to bring anything?"

I chuckled. "No. Just let me know when you're on the way."

"I got you."

We ended the call, and I went back to cooking. Without realizing it, the call from Ace was what I needed to put myself in a good mood. This thing with Ace and I was new, but one thing was for sure, he was a breath of fresh air. Fresh air I didn't know I needed.

Chapter Sixteen

Deandre 'Ace' Lemetti

I pulled up to my mother's house shortly after one. Gabby had fallen asleep during the ride, so I knew she would be out for a while. Glancing in the driveway, I spotted Deanna's car parked there. I killed the engine, took Gabby out of her seat, and headed inside.

"Yo," I called out.

"Stop yelling like you pay bills here," my mother said coming around the corner.

"I do," I smiled as she whacked me with her hand towel before taking a sleeping Gabby from my arm.

"I just made some fresh lemonade. It's in the fridge."

Without speaking another word, I headed straight to the kitchen. I didn't give a damn who tried, nobody was touching my mama with her lemonade. I could legit drink that shit straight out of the pitcher. I grabbed a cup and the pitcher and filled the cup to the top before guzzling it down. I refilled it just as Deanna made her way into the kitchen.

"You gonna save some for somebody else?" she questioned as she sat at the table.

"Nah, drink water." She flipped me the bird.

"You hungry?" my mother asked, reappearing in the kitchen.

"Nah, we just ate not too long ago."

"You cooked?"

"Nah, Infinity did."

"Infinity?" my mom questioned.

"The woman who owns the daycare center, Ma," Deanna clarified.

"Yeah, her," I told them both as I glanced back and forth between the two of them. "What's the problem with that?"

"What's the deal between the two of you?" my mother questioned, leaning on the table.

I shrugged. "We're together."

"And she's ready for the fact that you come with a child?"

"Umm, I would think so seeing as how my child is technically what brought us together."

"What about Aaliyah?" my mother inquired.

"What about her?" Just the mention of her name had me ready to snap. I had to count to ten and remember I was speaking to my mother.

"She has no say?"

"Why would she?"

"Give her a chance, Deandre."

"A chance to do what? Walk out of my daughter's life again? Nah, I'm good."

"A chance to be a mother. She's young. She was probably scared. She seems like she is ready to try."

"You got that off of her showing up at her daughter's party a year later? Or are you a mind reader?"

My mother sighed. I wasn't sure why she even brought this up. It didn't matter how much she tried to push this Aaliyah idea, if I allowed it to happen, it would happen on my time and my time only.

"Be open-minded to it, Deandre. Don't hold this against her forever."

"Oh, you mean the same way she would hold it against me if I was a deadbeat? Yeah, a'ight." I put the pitcher back in the fridge, placed my cup in the sink, and kissed both my mother and Deanna on the forehead. "I'll be back."

I walked through the living room and kissed a sleeping Gabby before heading out the door. I climbed in my car and headed to the main spot to meet up with Los. I had to give it to my nigga, he had been holding me the fuck down. I reached into the center console and pulled out half of a blunt I had left in there yesterday. Sparking it up, I turned up the music, where Chamillionaire's *Sound of Revenge* album was in rotation. I nodded my head to the beat as I entered the highway ramp and pressed harder on the gas. It took me no time to pull up to our spot in Pawtucket.

Los' car was parked in front of the crib. One of the smartest things he suggested was to make this look like a regular crib and nobody was served out of there. We always kept a beater in the yard so that it looked as if someone actually lived there. Whenever we met here, we would spend at least an hour there.

I put the blunt out before killing the engine and heading inside. Los sat at the table with his phone playing music and his gun locked and loaded.

"What's good, nigga?" I reached over to give him a pound.

"Ain't shit. You already know."

I sat at the table next to him as he finished rolling his blunt. Once it was sealed, he handed it to me to light it and got up to head to the hall closet. He returned with a money-counting machine and a duffle bag on his shoulder. I stood and grabbed the two iPads that we kept here in the drawer. Los walked away to grab another two bags from the closet. With the blunt dangling from my mouth, I powered on the iPads, leaving them in airplane mode.

Without speaking another word, Los and I got to work. While I counted the money by hand, Los ran it through the money machines. To me, we couldn't be too sure, so it never hurt to count money two or three times. In this game, you always had a nigga or two that you try you. However, the team we had was solid. Los and I had built our team up from the ground up and there wasn't a nigga on our team that we didn't trust with our lives.

Four hours later, Los and I had counted over six hundred grand. I couldn't help but sit back and smile. I didn't consider myself rich, but I was a wealthy ass nigga. My daughter wouldn't want for a damn thing, and I knew it was time for me to start creating generational wealth. I needed my great-great-grandkids to be set. In my personal stash, I knew I was coming up on two million dollars, and I needed to start investing my shit so I could make more money in my sleep.

I wasn't one of those flashy ass niggas that looked like I had money. My house was in my mother's name, and that took a lot of convincing, seeing as how she didn't agree with my line of work. I had simple ass cars, and I only stepped out in high fashion when I was ready to make a statement. Other than that, I wore simple shit like Nike, Jordan, and True Religion. I was a simple ass nigga.

"You good?" Los questioned. "I was a little concerned yesterday when you fell through the club," he chuckled. I shook my head and washed my hands over my face. I didn't tell Los what had happened that led me to meet him at the club, I just told him I needed to clear my damn head.

"My baby mama popped up at my daughter's party tryna act like she was the mom of the year." Los started coughing as he had just inhaled the weed smoke.

"She did what?"

"My nigga, you heard me. Turns out she hit up my sister, and

Deanna's rock-head ass thought it was okay to tell her to show up. Now my mother and Deanna are on my ass about letting her be part of my daughter's life. It's like they want me to forget about the fact that my daughter was left outside like yesterday's trash by a bitch who wanted to party. I've been questioning if maybe I'm being too hard on Aaliyah," I shrugged and sighed.

"Nah, not for nothing. I don't blame you. I know how you and ol' girl had rocked. I know you told her that you would raise the child if she didn't want it, but she could have faced you like a woman and let you know that and not left her outside. That's some shit that I would have a problem with forever because that don't make no damn sense."

"That's my point, but these two got me second-guessing if I'm doing what's best for my daughter and shit."

"From day one, you've always had her best interest at heart. Keep doing what you feel is right and whoever doesn't agree with it, fuck 'em." I nodded in agreement. We chopped it up and smoked another blunt before Los and I dapped each other up and headed out. We made plans to meet the following day to pay the team and make sure everyone was good.

I headed back to my mother's crib and was sure to pull into the garage. Exiting the car, I grabbed the duffle bag and headed straight to the old bedroom I had there. Coming back downstairs, I heard the TV going and Gabby clapping toys together. I scooped her up and began smothering her with kisses.

"You staying for dinner?" my mother asked as she stood from

the couch.

"Nah, I already told Infinity that we're going by her place."

"Tell her don't be trying to steal my grandbaby from me," she laughed.

"I got you. Thanks for keeping an eye on Gabby for me," I told her as I picked up Gabby's toys.

"Anytime. You know I love my baby girl." She took Gabby from my arms and kissed her a few times before putting her on the floor. Within twenty minutes, Gabby and I were leaving my mother's and heading toward one of our favorite people.

Chapter Seventeen

Infinity Morrison

Just as I was mixing butter into my rice, my doorbell rang. I moved the rice off the eye, turned off the stove, and headed to the door. I couldn't help but smile when I saw Ace and Gabby standing there.

"Hey," I greeted them. I planted a kiss on Ace's lips and grabbed Gabby from his arms. She gave me a juicy, gummy smile. I squeezed her tightly, before placing her on the floor in the area where her toys were. I headed back into the kitchen to finish mixing my rice before I made a plate for Ace and I, along with a small bowl for Gabby. Just as I sat the bowls down, Ace stood up and headed into the kitchen. I watched him as he returned with a sippy cup for Gabby and two bottles of water for both me and him. We sat down, and this time, I grabbed his hands and said a prayer out loud.

"Amen," we said in unison.

"How was your day?" I questioned him as we started to eat.

"It was cool. I handled what I needed to handle. My mom and sister got to spend time with Gabby. Seems like a win-win for me. How about you?"

"I got some housework done. I've been home since I left your house earlier."

We continued to make small talk as we finished dinner. I couldn't help but laugh when I saw Gabby was damn near wearing the rice and meat.

"Can you ever just eat without making a mess?" he asked her as he tried to wipe the food off her body before taking her out of her chair. "Do you have clothes here for her?"

"Of course." I headed toward my room to grab a diaper, wipes, and pajamas for Gabby. I handed them to Ace and told him to give her a bath while I cleaned up the kitchen. I couldn't stop the smile that spread across my face. Never did I imagine dating a child at my center's parent, but now that I had, I didn't regret it.

"What you over here smiling about?" Ace questioned, scaring me. I didn't even hear him come back.

"Just thinking."

"About?"

"Us."

"What about us?"

"Just how we became one," I shrugged. He walked up behind me and wrapped his arms around me as he snuggled his face in my neck. "You gave Gabby a bath that quick?"

"Shit, she dozed before I even made it upstairs. I wiped her down and changed her before she was out. I put her in your bed and propped the pillows around her," he explained. I nodded. He started planting soft kisses along my neck and jawbone. I couldn't help the shutter that my body let off. It had been a long time since I had a man's touch. I dropped the dish I had in my hand into the sink and threw my head back.

He ran his hands up and down the front of my body and I would be lying if I said I wasn't heating up. He reached over and shut the water off, before turning me around to face him. He stared into my eyes as he leaned toward me, mashing his lips against mine. He slipped his hands under my shirt, rubbing up and down my back. He moved his lips from mine and went straight back to my neck. My love canal was dripping, and my heart was racing. His hands crept up until he reached my bra hook. Like a pro, he unhooked my bra and ran his hands up to my arms to remove it. I closed my eyes to mentally prepare myself for what was about to happen. I was only nervous because of how long it had been since I had sex.

He lifted me and sat me on the counter as he moved his lips back to mind. My breathing became heavy, and Ace noticed it.

"You okay?" he questioned. I swallowed hard and nodded my head. "Do you want me to stop?" I quickly shook my head no. The site of his bulging member had me ready to risk it all. I placed my hands on the hem of his shirt and slowly raised it so he could remove it. Our eyesight never broke. Ace was fit as fuck and I almost wanted to lick him up and down. I licked my lips and tucked my bottom lip between my teeth. I reached for his waist to unbutton his jeans. Due to the weight of his wallet and phone, his pants dropped to the floor immediately. His dick was damn near at attention.

I hopped down off the counter and grabbed his hand to lead him to my spare bedroom. The moment we crossed the threshold, I pushed him down on the queen-sized bed I had there. Once he sat down, I straddled his lap and kissed him deeply. We fell backward without breaking the kiss in the process. His hands ran down my body and to the shorts that I had on. He slipped his hands into my shorts and began squeezing my ass. In one swift motion, he flipped me over to where he was now on top of me. His fingers quickly found my panties, and I knew they were soaking wet.

"Damn, ma. Tell me you were wanting this without telling me you were wanting this," he joked as he flicked at my nub. My eyes rolled in the back of my head as he began massaging and applying pressure to my button. I dug my nails into his back as I felt the almost forgotten tingle coming from my toes. I squeezed my thighs tighter. "Open up, shorty," Ace spoke low in my ear.

I released the breath I didn't realize I was holding. Ace removed his hands from my panties and slid down my body. He made his way down and slowly removed my shorts and panties simultaneously. Looking at me, he smirked before dipping his head between my awaiting pussy. He flicked his tongue across my bud, and I shuttered again. I gripped the back of his head and held him in place as he found the hidden spot above my clit that sent me over. Once he felt me tighten my legs, he attacked that spot and it wasn't long before I was crying out and cumming all over his face. As if he was dehydrated, he slurped up everything I released. My button was sensitive, but he kept at it. Within five minutes, I was experiencing another orgasm. With his beard and mouth glistening, Ace stood up and removed his boxers. He gave me a sexy grin before he climbed back onto the bed on top of me.

"You ready for this?" he asked. I nodded. "Once I dive into this, there is no turning back." I chuckled.

"I'm grown. I know what I'm doing," I told him. Without warning, he plunged deeply into me, taking my breath away in the process.

"Fuuuuck," he groaned as he paused. "Gah damn. I was not expecting this." After a few seconds, he began to slow stroke. The pain I once felt was quickly replaced by pleasure. Ace nuzzled his face into my neck again and I was back to digging into his back. Before I knew it, he flipped back over and had me on top. "Come on, gangsta. Show me how *grown* you truly are," he urged, using my words against me. Feeling inexperienced, I began to slow grind on him. Truthfully, I had no idea what the fuck I was doing, but I wasn't going to tell him that. I thought back to the porn videos I had watched. I planted my hands flat on

Ace's chest and got into a squatting position. Squatting flat on my feet with my hands planted, I began to bounce slowly. I was sure that Ace could sense my inexperience, but I appreciated him not pointing it out.

Ace gripped my hips and began to move me to the rhythm he wanted me to move. He matched my movements before he flipped me back over and had me on all fours. He slipped his dick back inside and went to pound town. He found my g-spot and began attacking it as if his life depended on it.

"Oh, shit," I panted. "I-I'm about to…" I couldn't finish my sentence as my eyes rolled, my walls clamped down on his dick, and I let loose. I collapsed on the bed as Ace continued stroking.

"Come on, mama. Don't quit on me now. I can tell she's backed up, so let me get her right," he growled lowly. I was spent and could easily curl up and pass out, but I could feel his dick was still hard. He tooted my ass up in the air slightly before gripping my hips and continuing to stroke. "I promise, one more and I'll let you be done."

I figured he was lying, but he was definitely waking me back up. I got back up on all fours and started throwing it back on him.

"Whoa," I heard him say. I couldn't help but smirk as I knew I was getting him. I began matching him stroke for stroke. "Slow down, ma." I ignored him and kept up with him. "Shit, I'm about to bust," I remembered the Kegels exercises I used to always do and began squeezing my walls, tightening myself around him.

"Fuuuuuuck," he groaned as he sped up. "Cum with me, shorty."

He made sure to locate my spot again, and before I knew it, that tingle was coming over me. My body slightly shuttered as I heard him groan before he pulled out, and my ass was covered in his nut. That was it. I was done. I literally felt drained.

"Yo shorty, that shit was wild as fuck. Damn." He walked out of the room; I'm assuming heading as I attempted to catch my breath. He returned a few moments later , and I felt a warm rag over my ass cheeks. Once he was done, I finally climbed out of bed and headed to the bathroom to take a shower. I turned on the shower and sat on the toilet to release my bladder. Ace appeared in the doorway in his boxers.

"You good?" he questioned with a chuckle.

"I think so."

"You weren't lying about not being with anybody for a while, huh?"

"You thought I was?" I snapped back.

"Nah, that's not what I meant. Your shit felt almost virgin-tight. I felt like I was busting through virgin walls all over again." I couldn't help but laugh and shake my head. "I gotta run to my crib because I realized I don't have any clothes."

"Okay." He walked over and planted a kiss on my lips followed by my forehead before heading out. I heard him close the door as I stood and climbed into the shower. I allowed the hot water to run down my body before removing the shower head, switching to the massager, and facing it toward my kitty. I was sore as fuck, but I wasn't complaining. After being in the shower for more than twenty minutes and washing up twice, I climbed out and wrapped myself in a towel. I went back into my room, grabbed my phone, and put the 90s R&B station on Pandora. Tossing the phone on my bed, I began to lather my body in lotion before grabbing panties and a nightgown. Just as I was about to pull the blanket back and climb into bed, I heard the doorbell go off. Snatching my phone, I checked the cameras at the front door and spotted Ace standing there with a duffle bag.

I rushed down the stairs to let him in. He followed me back upstairs and dropped his bag once he crossed the bedroom threshold.

"You showered at home?" I asked.

"Yeah. I just brought some random shit to keep here." I smirked and cocked my head to the side.

"Who told you I had room for your shit?" I joked.

"If you don't, you better make room for my shit." I tossed the pillow at his head before I plugged my phone in and climbed into bed. "My mom wants you to come by for dinner."

"Oh."

"Oh? That's all you can say?" He questioned.

"What am I supposed to say? I mean outside of the pickups at daycare, we haven't interacted," I shrugged.

"That's why she wants you to come by for dinner." I didn't miss the way his face twisted when he spoke. I sighed and shook my head. "A'ight, forget it."

"I don't mean it like that. From what I've seen of her between the daycare and Gabby's party, she seems like a nice person, but..."

"But what?"

"Nothing. Just let me know when and where."

"Nah, speak what's on your mind. You're grown, right? Act like it."

"Excuse me?"

"You heard me. Speak up."

"First of all, I have nothing against going to your mother's for dinner but excuse me for being nervous because I know she's going to fuckin' drill me," I snapped. "I can hold my own, but it's been a long ass time since I've had to impress someone's mother."

"Who said you had to impress her? Just be yourself."

I shook my head because his ass just wouldn't get it.

"Just forget it." I climbed out of bed and walked away because the last thing I wanted to do was stand here and argue with him. Ace and I had just had a nice night and I didn't want to ruin it. I didn't want him to think that I didn't want to go to his mother's home, because I would love to. I just wanted to make sure that everyone was ready for that. I returned a few minutes later, and Ace looked like he was still sitting there with an attitude. I wasn't one who liked to go to bed mad, so I sighed and then looked at him before speaking. I climbed back into bed and sat propped up against the headboard.

"Listen, like I said, I would love to gather with your family. Please don't think that I don't want to. I just don't want you to think that you have to rush to do it if you're not ready."

"If I wasn't ready for it, I wouldn't have mentioned it. Nobody can make me do things that I don't want to do. You're important to me, and it's only right that the women who are important to me gather together and hit it off. If I thought y'all wouldn't get along, I probably wouldn't have pursued you, and I damn sure wouldn't have suggested going to her house for dinner."

"So your mom determines who you date?"

"Are you going to find an argument in everything?" he asked. I threw my hands up and sighed.

"Okay, never mind. Again, just let me know when and where." I leaned over and kissed his cheek before he turned and brought his lips to mine. "Goodnight." I handed him the remote and slid down before tucking the blanket under my chin. It didn't take me long to fall asleep, and something told me this would be some of the best sleep I had gotten in a while.

Chapter Eighteen

Deandre 'Ace' Lemetti

I stretched and rubbed my eyes before looking around the unfamiliar room. Taking a moment, I quickly remembered that we had spent the night with Infinity. I smirked and rolled over, only to find her side of the bed empty. I laid there silent for a second to see if I could hear anything, but the house was quiet. I climbed out of bed and headed to the bathroom to handle my hygiene and release my bladder. Once I was done, I headed back to Infinity's room to grab my phone. The moment I illuminated the phone, my eyes almost popped out of my head when I saw it was after ten in the morning. An unopened text from Infinity sat on my lock screen.

Infinity: (5:45 AM) – By the time you see this, Gabby and I will already be at the center. I didn't want to wake you up so early because it looked like you were finally getting a good night's rest. I'm not sure what you have to do today, but I hope you have a good day.

She closed the message out with a heart and kissy face emoji. I smiled and tapped her name to call her. I sat on the side of the bed as I listened to the phone ring.

"Hello."

"What's up, beautiful? How's your day going?"

"Hey. Not too bad so far. You're just getting up?"

"Yeah."

"Just as I suspected, you needed that rest," she chuckled.

"You still could have woken me up."

"It's okay."

"How was Gabby with getting up that early?" I asked as I grabbed my duffle bag to pull out something to wear.

"She didn't," she chuckled again. "I got her dressed while she was sleeping. She actually woke up shortly after we got here to the center, and she was fine then."

Before I could say anything else, my phone beeped, signaling an incoming call. I didn't recognize the number, so I let it roll over to voicemail.

"Do you want me to pick her up before the center closes?"

"Doesn't matter."

"A'ight. I'll let you know." My phone began beeping again with the same number calling. "Let me hit you back. I have another call coming in, and I have no idea who it is."

"Okay. Have a good day."

"You too, Ma."

She hung up, and I answered the incoming call.

"Yo," I snapped.

"Ace?"

"Who's this?"

"Aaliyah."

The phone went silent. I had to take a few deep breaths and even ran my tongue across my teeth. This girl was pushing my damn buttons, and the harder she pushed to try and force her way into my daughter's life, the more I wanted her to stay away.

"What, man? What the fuck do you want?"

"I...I just want to talk."

"How did you even get my number?"

She didn't say anything, and I wouldn't have been surprised if she said Deanna.

"We don't even have shit to talk about," I continued.

"Yes, we do. We have a daughter."

"No, I have a daughter."

"Deandre, she's my daughter too," she cried.

"Oh, now she's your daughter? Who was she to you when you left her on the porch without even having the balls to ring the doorbell?" She didn't respond, but I could hear her sniffling. "Exactly what the fuck I thought. Go back to doing whatever the fuck you've been doing for the last year."

I ended the call before she could respond and immediately blocked her number. I opened my text thread with Deanna and shot her a message.

Me: (10:23 AM) – Did you give Aaliyah my number?

I prayed she would say no because I truly would hate to have to cut my sister off. I loved her ass to death and the last thing I wanted to do was be on the outs with her. That shit would kill me slowly.

I tossed my phone on the bed as I pulled my sweats up over my lower body. I grabbed a T-shirt and put it on before doing the same with my socks and shoes. For a split second, I thought about trying to put my shit away, but I knew females were particular about their shit, and I didn't want to get her shit all mixed up and have to hear about it later. I pushed the bag against the wall, grabbed my phone, keys, and wallet, and headed out. I realized I would only be locking her knob. I dialed up Infinity again as I stood in her doorway.

"Hey."

"Hey, how do you want me to lock up? Just the knob?"

"Yeah, that's fine. I have cameras all around my house, so I'll be able to see if anything happens."

"A'ight. I'm heading out for a few. If you want something for lunch, let me know."

"I haven't thought about it yet, but I'll let you know."

"A'ight."

We ended the call, and my phone vibrated, letting me know a message was coming through. I saw it was Deanna and opened it immediately.

Deanna (10:40 AM) – No, I wouldn't go that far in doing

that.

I didn't bother to respond because Aaliyah was notorious for doing some crazy shit. I brushed it off and left it alone. I pulled out my burner and dialed up Los as I pulled out of Infinity's driveway.

"Yo," he answered.

"You at the spot?"

"Yessir."

"Bet. I'll meet you."

We ended the call, and I headed to Los' spot. I didn't bother to turn the music on as I used the drive to let my mind run free. So much had happened within the last year, and it was still hard for me to believe it. I sighed heavily as this situation with Aaliyah weighed heavily on my mind. My mother was no help, and neither was Deanna. Infinity would agree with whatever I decide to do. In times like this, I wish my grandmother was still alive or my father. I shook my head lightly as I pulled up to Los' spot. I spotted his car in the driveway. Killing the engine, I headed to the side door and let myself in.

"Yo, yo," I called out.

"Yerrr," he responded.

He met me in the living room and dapped me up.

"What's good with you?"

"Shit, man. Same shit, different day."

"I hear that." I followed Los into his basement. "How shit been?"

"For the most part, it's cool. One of the spots came up short last week, but I'm about to recount to double-check."

"Short?" I questioned. "Which one?"

"West End."

"Shit, that's the top spot. Short by how much?"

"Twenty."

"Nah, ain't no way your count is off by twenty bands." I pulled the chair out and sat at the table as Los tossed the duffle bag on the table. He grabbed a money counter that he kept here, and I immediately started counting by hand. At that moment, I zoned in and focused only on making sure I was accurate. Just as I finished each stack, I wrote down the number, and Los ran it through the machine. Just as he said, the count was twenty thousand dollars short. I would be lying if I said my blood wasn't boiling. I treated everyone fairly and paid everyone right, so stealing was an ultimate fuckin' no in my book.

"Am I trippin', or nah?"

"Nah, you ain't, but them niggas are. Get them niggas to the spot ASAP," I snapped. I began pacing his basement as I tried to calm down. One thing I hated was a thief, and with the way I handled business, I felt like the last thing anyone in my camp should have been was a thief.

"I got you. Chill. We're gonna handle this shit," Los let me know, but I wasn't trying to hear it. Los pulled out his burner and I knew he was moving some men around and calling an immediate meeting. "What time you want to do it?"

"After sunset. I gotta make sure my daughter is down and taken care of but definitely tonight."

"Bet. We can link at ten."

"A'ight. How did that delivery go?" I questioned regarding our recent re-up that he handled.

"Shit was smooth. Everything is ready for distro this weekend." I nodded. "Here, fire this up," Los said. I looked over and saw he was holding out a blunt. I immediately grabbed it and wasted no time firing it up. I needed something to calm my nerves because I didn't want to react on impulse. It seemed as if I was being tested from all angles, but one thing was for sure. I hadn't folded to date, and I wasn't about to start now. Once I finished smoking with Los, I checked the time and saw it was just after noon. Infinity hadn't texted me regarding lunch, so I decided to just order a large wing order for the staff at the center. I shot her a text and let her know that I had lunch covered for her staff.

I dapped Los up just as I dialed up the bar to place the order. I headed toward the gas station to top off my tank, grab a few drinks, and then to the bar to grab the food. Once I had the order, I headed up the street to the daycare center just as my phone rang. Looking at the Bluetooth screen on my dash, I saw it was Infinity.

"What's up, mama?"

"Hey, where are you?"

"Pulling up."

"Okay, I'll unlock the doors." She ended the call just as I parked. As I climbed out of the car, I spotted her waiting at the door. She came out toward me and began grabbing the drinks out of the car. "You didn't have to do this," she said just before she planted a kiss on my lips.

"You tell me that every time I do something, and I repeat myself each time. I know I don't have to, but I will." She blushed and turned around heading back inside. I followed her inside and went into the conference room where we placed everything on the tables. She went into the cabinet and grabbed a stack of paper plates, napkins, and cups.

"Sit with me," she said as she started popping the lids on the containers. "You look like you have the weight of the world on your shoulders again. What's going on?"

I sighed and sat in the chair. She made herself a plate, made me a plate, and closed the door before she sat across from me. I looked at her but didn't say anything.

"Don't look at me like that. You wear your stress on your face. Talk to me." She picked up a piece of chicken and bit into it without taking her eyes off me. I washed my hands down my face and sighed before I gave her the soft version of what was happening. I told her about someone in my crew stealing from me to the uneasy feeling I was getting from Aaliyah. I was getting a nagging feeling that she wasn't going to go away easily, but little did she know, behind Gabrielle, I would go to war with guns blazing. "Have you considered actually giving her a chance?" she questioned.

"I have. I've actually thought about it several times. It's just every time I think about her, I'm brought back to that day of finding my daughter on the porch, and honestly, that's some shit I'm struggling to get over. I'll be honest. I don't know shit about being a father, and if I didn't have my moms, Deanna, and now you, I probably would be fuckin' up ten times worse. What makes me better than her?" I asked truthfully.

"What makes you better is the fact that rather than running, you adjusted. To yourself, you may not consider yourself to be the best father, but to Gabby, you're her knight and shining armor. You're the only parent she knows. It's a good thing you have a support system because everyone needs one. Not everyone has a good parental figure, but Gabby has one. She's young, so you still have time to make the necessary changes you feel you need to make to be better for not only you but for her. As far as her mother, like I told you before, only you know exactly what to do for the sake of your daughter. Think about it, pray about it, and whatever decision you make, do it with an open mind."

I smirked at her as I looked into her eyes.

"I'm glad my mama forced me to bring Gabby here," I admitted. She twisted her face as she chewed her food.

"What do you mean?"

"When I first got Gabby, my mom was keeping her for me. She told me that she had to get back to work, so I had to put her in daycare. She came across your Facebook post about you opening your center. I had no idea where to even look, let alone how to set up a child for daycare, but I'm glad it all worked out and she's here."

She blushed, finished eating, and wiped her hands on a napkin before she walked over and sat on my lap.

"I'm glad she did too," she said before planting a soft kiss on my lips. "And I'm glad I met you too." She tapped the tip of my nose before laughing.

"Don't do that corny shit again," I told her as I chuckled and patted her thighs. "Gabby sleeping?" I questioned.

"Probably because that girl don't play about her naps." I smiled at her statement. I pulled her close to me and nuzzled my nose into her neck, inhaling her scent. "How long is your lunch?" I asked.

"I usually take about an hour," she said.

"Bet, come on." I tapped her leg, causing her to stand up. I grabbed her hand and led her to her office. Along the way, I looked around to make sure nobody was coming toward us. When we entered her office, I closed and locked the door.

"What are you doing?" she asked.

"Having lunch." I pulled her over to the small couch that she had.

"Wait."

"Hush. Just keep it down and feed your nigga." I pulled her onto my lap and ran my hands up and down her back as I nestled my face into her neck and began softly sucking on it. She threw her head back as she ran her hands over my head. I could feel her breathing picking up. I let my hands roam down to the top of her pants before I started tugging at the hem. I lifted her up so I could pull them over her ass. I softly paced kisses along her stomach. Once her pants were down, she stepped out of them. I laid back on the couch and she straddled over me. I could see her breathing heavily. I readjusted her so that her pussy was directly on my mouth. I could hear the gasp she let out as I made love to her pearl. I separated her lips with my tongue and pulled her bud between my teeth. I could hear her moaning and I knew she was trying to stifle the sound.

I then placed my tongue on the spot right above her bulb and feverishly began to vibrate my tongue against it, causing her to grip the couch tightly and try and close her legs. I kept my hands planted on her thighs so she wouldn't suffocate me. It wasn't long before her legs began to shake violently. I lapped up every drop of her juices as she whimpered. Once I licked her clean, I lifted her as I sat up. I attempted to place her on her feet, but her legs were unsteady. I chuckled as I sat up straight and sat her on the couch next to me as she caught her breath. I looked down and my dick was bulging. I was tempted to catch a quickie, but I knew after that, she would be ready to leave for the day.

"You have anything to clean up with in here?" I asked her. She pointed to her desk.

"I have a small pack of wipes in my purse, which is in my

bottom drawer." Her eyes were closed as she spoke. I went around and grabbed her wipes and proceeded to clean her up before she put her pants back on. Once she was fully dressed, I kissed her deeply.

"Go ahead and get back to work. I'll be here to get her on time. I gotta make a few moves later on tonight, and I gotta spend some time with my baby girl before then."

"Okay. Be careful."

I stood up and pulled her into my embrace before planting a kiss on her forehead.

"Of course. Don't work too hard." I headed toward the door with Infinity in tow and she watched as I headed to the car. One thing was for sure, Infinity was different, but I wasn't lying when I told her I was glad Gabby ended up there. I could see myself falling in love with that damn girl and I would be lying if I said I would try and stop that from happening.

Chapter Nineteen

Aaliyah Murphy

I sighed heavily as I dropped my phone back into my scrubs after trying to dial Ace's number again. It was clear that he had blocked me, but I held on to a small piece of hope that he would unblock me. It was killing me that he wasn't open to allowing me back into her life. He wasn't even giving me a chance to show him that I had changed. I dropped my head into my hands and tried to think of what I could do to get back into my daughter's life. I was trying to avoid the court route because I knew it could be messy as hell, and costly, but I was almost desperate.

If I could go back to that day, I would have at least had a conversation with Ace. I'm sure he would have been a lot more accepting if I had just spoken to him about what I was going through. I didn't realize I had been crying until I opened my eyes and saw the puddle on the table. I wiped my face, took a deep

157

breath, cleaned the table, and headed back to finish my shift. I loved my job because I grew a love for helping people, but the parts I hated were watching parents come in with their children while I was damn near on my knees begging to be back with mine. I didn't regret much in life, but this was one thing I definitely did regret.

Thankfully, the remainder of my shift went by quickly. After work, I headed home to shower and change. Once I was dressed, I grabbed my keys and headed out so I could go to Walmart and re-up on the things I needed. I prayed the store wasn't crowded, but I mentally prepared myself that it was. Once inside, I began browsing the aisles and thought I was seeing things when I spotted the lady I saw sitting with Ace at Gabby's party. For some reason, my heart started racing. Before I could stop myself, I was walking in her direction. She was smiling and started talking and that was when I realized she had an AirPod in her ear. Part of me wanted to walk away, but another part of me wanted to seize the opportunity.

"Okay. Okay, I'll call you when I'm on the way. Alright, bye." She smiled as she tapped her AirPod.

"Excuse me," I called out to get her attention. She snapped her head in my direction and offered me a small smile, yet I realized she looked nervous.

"Yes?"

"I'm sorry. I know this is weird, but I just...I'm desperate and need your help," I admitted. I felt vulnerable, but I wasn't lying when I said I was desperate. I was yearning for time with my daughter, and as the days went on, it was getting harder and harder.

"My help? I'm sorry, do I know you?"

"My name is Aaliyah. You don't know me, and you probably never heard of me. I just remember seeing you at my daughter's birthday party and you looked like you knew her dad," I sighed because I couldn't believe I even had to go through this. "I've been trying to reach out to Ace to become involved in our daughter, Gabrielle's life and he's just not trying to hear me out. I was just wondering if you could maybe talk to him and try and convince him to at least give me a chance."

Tears welled in my eyes because I knew she was looking at me like I was crazy as hell, but I didn't care. I would try any and everything and I made a vow that if this didn't work, then I would go to the courthouse.

"I...Uh, wow. I'm sorry. You've taken me by surprise. So let me get this right." She shifted her weight from one foot to another. "You want me to try and convince Ace to talk to you?" For a brief moment, I was going to catch an attitude because I felt like she was judging me. I didn't know how much she knew about me and Ace's situation, but I wasn't feeling the way she was looking at me.

"You know what," I pursed my lips together and gave her a forced smile. "Forget it. I'm sorry for even bothering you." I backed up and turned around to walk away. I shook my head and took a deep breath.

"I'll let him know," she called out. "I hope it all works out for you."

I stopped in my tracks, closed my eyes, smiled, and sighed.

"Thank you," I said over my shoulder before I continued on my shopping trip. I was sure Ace wouldn't have approved of the way I went about reaching out to him, but at this point, it was what it was.

*****

I hummed softly to the music that played as I scooped a heaping mound of spaghetti onto my plate. I sprinkled Parmesan cheese on top and grabbed the garlic bread from out of the oven. I took a slice, grabbed a bottle of water, and headed into the living room to catch up on my shows. Just as I sat down, my phone began vibrating on the coffee table. Picking it up, I had to double-take when I saw Ace was calling me. I was hesitant to answer, but this is ultimately what I was waiting for.

"Hello," I answered before the voicemail picked up.

"What?"

"Excuse me?"

"You out here blowing up my line, and you stopping people and asking for me and shit, so what? What the fuck do you want?"

"Why do you have to be so nasty?" My lip quivered, but I refused to let him hear me cry. It was hard to believe that two years ago this man loved the hell out of me, but now acted as if I was the scum of the earth.

"You know what I want, Deandre. I just want to be part of my daughter's life."

"Why?"

"Why? What do you mean why? I'm her mother."

"Since when?"

I was blown away at the disrespect and my hurt was turning into anger.

"I may not have been there, and I may not have made the right decisions, but it doesn't change the fact that she's my child as well. I've changed, Deandre. I just want a chance to make it right. I can't make up for the last year that I've missed of her life, but I want to be there moving forward. Why are you making this hard?"

"I'm making it hard? You didn't fuckin' want her, remember? You left her outside like yesterday's fuckin' trash! And for what? So you can club hop and thot with a bunch of bitches that never gave a fuck about you? You made shit this way, Aaliyah! I'll give it to you, you gave it a shot, but you ultimately made the decision to walk away. If it was me that walked away, you would never let me back into her life. You would be calling me every deadbeat ass nigga in the world. I would have to jump through hoops to even see her, but because it's you, and you're the *mother*, I should just open up and let you in? Nah, fuck that shit. I move to the beat of my own drum. When I'm good and ready, if I ever even get to that point, I'll let you know. If you indeed did change, then good for you. I'm happy for you, but I gotta protect my daughter because you failed to do that shit. Stop blowing up my line and stop asking people about me. I'm good and my daughter is good. Stop tryna force shit."

Before I could say anything else, the phone beeped in my ear letting me know he had hung up.

"Ughhhh!" I shouted as I tossed my phone onto the table. I was done playing nice. I fucked up, and I understood that, but I was tired of him throwing that shit in my face. Bitches did worse all the time, but at least I made sure my daughter was good before I took off. That deserved credit too, right?

I sat on the couch fuming. I lost my appetite, but I knew I needed to eat. At that point, I was done playing with Ace. If he wanted to play, then it was game on. I tried to work with him, but since he refused, I could go the legal way. Whatever the cost would be, I would chalk it up. My daughter was worth that and so much more.

Chapter Twenty

Infinity Morrison

I watched as Ace paced back and forth, and for a second, I regretted telling him that his baby's mother had approached me. One thing I can say is she indeed did look remorseful, but I also didn't know the girl. I listened to their conversation since he had the phone on speaker and vowed at that moment, I was staying out of it. Something in me told me this was going to get messy. I understood Ace's point of view, but I could also understand Gabby's mom wanting just a chance. I had zoned out and didn't realize that Ace had stopped pacing until he plopped on the couch next to me and threw his head back.

"Why the fuck do I have to be the one placed in this situation?" he questioned to nobody in particular.

"Because God knew you would make the right decision. Right now, it seems like it's the end of the world, but you'll get through it," I tried to assure him.

He sighed. "I damn sure hope so."

"I know you said you had something to do, so I won't hold you. I just wanted to stop by and tell you what happened," I told him, standing to leave. I saw him lift his arm and check the time.

"Do you want to go with us to Chuck E. Cheese? I figured we could go there for like an hour or so to get her tired before I drop her off at my moms for the night," he said.

"Sure, if you want me to," I shrugged.

"Shit, if it were up to me, you would be with me all the damn time. However, I know you have a life, too," he laughed. I smiled as I slipped my feet into my flats. Gabby was sitting on the floor playing with her blocks. I scooped her up and planted kisses all over her face as she let out giggles.

"Come on, girlfriend. Let's get your jacket on so we can head out," I spoke to her as I headed to where I knew her room was. Within five minutes, we were heading back to the living room. I grabbed the diaper bag that was sitting on the kitchen chair before Ace took her from me. I walked out the door with the two of them following me.

Within a half hour, we were pulling into the Chuck E. Cheese parking lot. I shook off my jacket to prepare myself to chase Gabby through this place.

"Getting comfortable?" he questioned.

"I don't expect your big ass to chase her through this place," I laughed.

"Shit, you got that right. I'm just here to provide the funds."

"Simple ass," I smiled. "Let's go." We both climbed out, and he grabbed Gabby from her seat. We headed inside, and thankfully, the place wasn't too crowded. Gabby immediately started bouncing up and down in Ace's arms in excitement. "Somebody is ready to run," I spoke as we got our hands stamped and walked to the counter for a play card.

"Welcome to Chuck E. Cheese. How can I help you?" the hostess greeted.

"Shit, I don't know what you want to get. Go ahead and pick whatever you want. Order some pizza and shit," Ace told me. I shook my head, selected the amount of time we wanted to play, and ordered a pizza and a pitcher of juice while removing Gabby's jacket. Ace paid as I put Gabby on the floor, and she wasted no time taking off. I couldn't help but laugh as I chased behind her as she ran to the first machine.

"Wait, Gabby," I laughed. "We gotta get the card from daddy." I scooped her up and walked back over to where I spotted Ace putting the stuff down. He slid back into the booth as we walked up and grabbed the card. "We'll be back."

I placed Gabby on the floor and let her take off. I had to admit; I had a blast chasing her around. Moving from game to game and watching the excitement was enough satisfaction for me. Out of the corner of my eye, I saw the staff placing the pizza on the table where Ace was sitting.

"Come on, let's go eat." I guided Gabby to the bathroom to

wash her hands before we went to the table to meet Ace. As we were approaching the table, I spotted a female talking to Ace, and based on the look on his face, he wasn't happy. I picked up Gabby and put her inside of the booth, completely ignoring the female. I grabbed a plate and put a slice of pizza on it for Gabby to eat.

"Is this you and Aaliyah's baby?" the woman asked. I quickly looked up at Ace who looked as if he had smoke coming from his ears.

"Nah, that's my daughter. Fuck do you want Amanda?" he snapped. I nudged him under the table and quickly shook my head no slightly. I didn't know who this woman was, but the last thing I wanted him to do was to create an entire scene in this spot. It wasn't worth it.

"I was just saying hi."

"Well, you said hi. Now, why are you still here?"

"Ew, your attitude is nasty."

"Ain't shit changed. I ain't fuck with you when I was with Aaliyah, and I ain't about to fuck with you now. You could have acted like you ain't see me and kept it pushing. Ain't shit over this way for you, and I highly doubt you're looking for Aaliyah. You'll know how to contact her before I would," he said before turning his body straight to get a slice of pizza. I looked up at the woman and didn't miss the dirty look she gave me. I was tempted to say something, but she walked off before I could even open my mouth.

166

"Who was that?" I questioned.

"One of Aaliyah's friends she used to run the streets with. Ain't spoke to her ass since before Aaliyah even got pregnant, so I have no idea why she even felt the need to stop and speak to me," he shrugged.

I scoffed but didn't say anything. Instead, I helped Gabby eat her food and remained silent. I could feel Ace staring at me, but I refused to make eye contact.

"What's up?" he questioned.

"With what?"

"Your attitude."

"I'm good," I told him.

"Sell that bullshit to someone else. I can read it all over your face that you have a problem. You said we aren't doing the being mad at each other and shit, so talk about it."

I sighed and shook my head. Gabby's mother was becoming a thorn in my side, and I didn't know anything about her besides her damn name. The shit was getting old and fast.

"Oh, so that's how it's gonna be? A'ight, bet."

I sat silently for a few moments before I spoke up without looking at him.

"What's truly her issue with you?" I asked.

"Who's issue with me?"

"Your baby's mother."

"Shit if I know." He sat back, sighed, and looked at me. "No, I'm not fuckin' her. No, I don't want to be with her. No, I have never led her on. No, to any other wild ass question you may have. She literally shut me out midway through her pregnancy. I didn't even know if she carried the pregnancy to term. I had no idea the gender of my child until my neighbor rang my doorbell the day she was dropped on my porch. I wish her ass would have stayed gone. The last year without her has been peaceful, but ever since she popped up, it's been a nightmare.

"I damn sure haven't spoken to any of her people since she shut me out. I figured they knew where she was and refused to tell me, so I said fuck them all," he shrugged.

"Okay."

"That's it? That's all you have to say?"

"What else do you want me to say? You explained, so there's nothing additional to say."

"Yeah, but the vibe you're giving is saying something else."

"I've never been in a situation like this, so I'm trying to tread lightly. I..."

"What's good, Infinity?" I heard someone speak. My head snapped to my right, and at that moment, I wished I hadn't.

"Jermaine."

"You look good. No love?" he questioned with his arms spread out.

"Uh...No. Good to see you," I told him and went back to focusing on Gabby.

"Damn, you wouldn't have a baby by me, but you had a baby by someone else," he chuckled. I froze. At that moment, every emotion I felt about losing my son came rushing back to me. Immediately, tears sprang to my eyes and raced down my cheeks.

"You good, mama?" I heard Ace ask, but I couldn't respond. Instead, I dropped the napkin I had in my hand, stood up, and rushed toward the door. I could hear Ace yelling after me, but I had to get away from everyone. Jermaine was a bad memory I wanted to forget. The pain he caused me was one I never wanted to experience again. Making a comment about not wanting to have a baby with him was a huge trigger because, little did he know, I wanted my son more than I wanted my next breath.

I walked around the building with my arms wrapped around my body. When I felt as though I was far enough away from the entrance, I sat on the curb and cried. I cried harder than I had in a long time. I cried for my son. I cried for the children I would likely never have. I cried just as hard as I did the day that they told me my son was gone. I was sure I looked ridiculous sitting here sobbing, but I was truly aching.

At this moment, I wished the ground would open up, swallow me, and bring me to my son. Life wasn't fair. To make matters worse, I noticed he was with his daughter's mother and their daughter.

"Mama," I heard. I lifted my head and saw Ace standing there with Gabby who looked at me with a gummy smile. I tried to match her smile, but I couldn't. It hurt too bad. "Come on, ma." He reached his hand out for me to place my hand in his. I shook my head no. It was rare I regretted being out somewhere, but right now, I was regretting coming to Chuck E. Cheese. I should have taken my ass home. "Come on," he repeated. "Let's get Gabby to my moms and we can talk, or you can let out all of your pain, and I'll just listen. Whatever you want to do."

I sniffled and wiped my face before grabbing his hand and standing up. He pulled me into his embrace, and I lost it again.

"I'm sorry. I shouldn't have come. I ruined your outing with your daughter. I'm sorry."

"Shh," he said. "You didn't ruin anything. That nigga, whoever he is, is the one with the issue. I don't like seeing you like this, and clearly, he's a problem. So you can tell me about him whenever you're ready."

I sniffled and slowly nodded. He grabbed my hand, and we walked over to his car. Gabby kept looking at me, and when we locked eyes, she smiled wide. I took Gabby from Ace and put her in the car. I planted a huge kiss on her cheek and told her that I loved her. I climbed into the front seat, took a deep breath, and leaned my head against the window.

In no time, we pulled up to what I assumed was his mother's house.

"Do you want to come in?" he asked. I shook my head. I know his mother wanted to meet me, but right now, I wanted nothing more than to go the hell home, climb in bed and stay there. Ace didn't push the issue. He grabbed Gabby with her bag and headed inside. While he was gone, I pulled out my phone and shot both Jas and Mel a text and let them know I was taking tomorrow off. The both of them had the code to unlock the center and knew exactly what needed to be done for it to run for the day, and I trusted them.

Within ten minutes, Ace returned, but I realized he wasn't alone. When he opened the door and the light came on, I noticed his mother was with him.

"I told her you weren't in the mood to come in, so she wanted to come out."

"Hi, nice to see you again," she smiled. "If you're free on Sunday, come by for dinner with this big-headed ass guy," she joked, pointing to Ace. "I would love to get to know you a little more." I couldn't help the smile that spread across my face.

"I don't think I have anything planned, so I'll be here." She smiled wider before standing up, kissing Ace on the cheek, and heading back inside. Ace climbed into the car before pulling off.

"My house or yours?" he questioned.

"My car is at your house, but I want to go home," I told him honestly. "I'll get my car tomorrow or something."

"Do I need to pick you up in the morning for work?" he asked.

"No, I told Jas and Mel I won't be there." He didn't say anything else as we made the short drive to my house. I closed my eyes and sent a silent prayer to my son. I couldn't wait to cross the threshold to my house because the first thing I was doing was running straight to him. I needed to feel him close to me at this point.

Chapter Twenty - One
Deandre 'Ace' Lemetti

My phone vibrated as I glanced down at Infinity who was now sleeping. Looking at the screen, I saw it was Los. I silenced the vibration as I slid out of the bed, careful not to wake Infinity. Once I was up, I took one more look at her before going out into the hall to return Los' call.

"Yo," he answered on the second ring.

"What's good?"

"Shit. Ready when you are."

"Bet. Give me twenty."

"Say less." We ended the call and I went back into Infinity's room to throw my clothes back on. I grabbed my black, mid-top AF1s and sat on the edge of the bed before putting them on. I felt Infinity shift behind me. I glanced over my shoulder and saw she was looking at me.

"You okay?" I asked her.

"Yeah. Where are you going?"

"I gotta go meet up with my partner. I shouldn't be long."

"Be careful." I could see she was slightly uneasy, but she wasn't going to put up a fight.

"Always."

Once I put my other shoe on, I stood and walked around to her side of the bed before planting a kiss on both her forehead and her lips.

"Take my key to let yourself back in."

"A'ight."

I grabbed her keys off the nightstand before taking one more look at her and heading out. My mind was all over the place as I headed to meet Los. For as long as I had been in this business, I never had to deal with a nigga on my team stealing from me, so it fucked with me heavy that niggas felt like they had to even stoop to that level. I gripped the steering wheel tighter and pressed my lips together to try and calm myself so I could go into this shit with a clear head.

It took me no time to pull up to the warehouse that we rarely visited but kept for instances like this. Niggas knew that if we had to come here, someone wasn't leaving here alive. I pulled up and killed the engine, before stepping out onto the dirt-filled road. I adjusted my sweats so that my gun remained on my hip. I glanced around to check my surroundings before walking inside. The heavy metal door slammed behind me, grabbing the attention of the niggas from my west side spot. I sighed heavily as I walked up and dapped up Los. I looked around the area as the six workers who rotated at the trap stared back at me.

"I'm sure y'all know why y'all are here," I voiced in an annoyed tone. "So I'll give y'all a chance to say what needs to be said before I say what the fuck I wanna say." I placed my gun on the table that sat in front of me and took a seat. They all looked around at each other before their eyes made their way back to me. "Nobody has nothing to say."

I noticed one of the niggas reaching down beside him. I immediately grabbed my piece from the table, cocked it, and aimed it at him. He threw his hands in the air in surrender looking scared shitless.

"Chill," he spoke, clearly nervous as hell. He slowly reached back down on his side before he returned his hand to view holding an envelope. "If this is what it's about, then here's what was given to me." I cocked my head to the side and placed the gun back down on the table.

"Explain."

I watched as he looked at the guys that he was sitting next to him, and they all shook their heads.

"I came into the spot one day and was told that our pay was being increased. I thought the shit was skeptical because it wasn't coming from y'all. It wasn't a large amount, so something told me to hold on to the shit. I'm glad I did," he shrugged as he tossed the envelope down the table. I looked at Los who picked it up and quickly skimmed through it.

"That's about five bands," he told me.

"So there's another fifteen bands missing." I turned my attention back to the guys at the table. Malachi, the one who slid the envelope down the table sat back and looked unphased. I didn't miss him shaking his head softly. I had to admit, what he did was some real shit and I respected him for it. I grabbed the envelope back from Los and slid it back to Malachi. "Keep that shit. I appreciate your honesty. You're excused."

He looked at me confused, but he stood up and walked out, leaving the envelope on the table. I knew he wasn't sure if I was actually testing him or not, but I meant what I said.

"Take it, Malachi," I told him before he made it out of the door. He looked back over his shoulder. "It's not a test. Consider it a token of appreciation. I'll holla at you." He walked back over to the table and grabbed the envelope before heading out. Once he was gone, I sat back and looked at the remaining five men. "I really don't have all night. So one of two things can happen. Either y'all can start fuckin' talking or everyone can be on the next missing poster. You got about thirty seconds to pick," I told them, meaning every single word I said. Truthfully, I wanted nothing more than to get back to Infinity and lay up under her.

The room remained silent. I nodded my head because clearly, I wasn't getting anywhere with these niggas.

"So, what would you do in my situation?" I questioned. He shrugged and dropped his head. "What would you do, Los?"

"Thieving ass niggas usually get put six feet deep with no

hesitation." He wasn't lying either. The game always made an example out of a nigga who stole, but something in me didn't want to put this nigga six feet deep. "What I really want to know is who one is who started this shit and why," Los said. He was speaking exactly what I was thinking. I personally felt like we took very good care of our workers, so it was more than a slap in the face for them to turn around and steal from us.

"I honestly don't have all fuckin' day to sit here. The same way y'all were quick to steal from me should be the same way y'all are quick to own up to it. I'm trying to give y'all asses the benefit of the doubt to at least be honest, but I feel like I'm wasting my fucking time," I snapped. "Somebody better get to talking before bullets get to flying." I picked up my piece again and cocked it, putting one in the chamber just in case I needed it.

"A'ight," the youngest cat Sly spoke up. Not only was he the youngest one, but he was also the newest. He reminded me a lot of myself. "I started the shit. I honestly didn't think y'all would notice. I know for a fact y'all bring in crazy money each week, so I damn sure didn't think y'all would notice or miss a weak ass twenty bands."

"Are you struggling?" Los questioned.

"I'm pretty sure we're all struggling, which is why we're

hustlin'," he responded.

"Speak for yourself. You can call it twenty weak-ass bands, but you took the bitch ass way out rather than just being upfront and asking for help. Tell me, though. Give me one good reason why I shouldn't pop your ass right now?" I gritted.

"Do what you gotta do," he shrugged. Before I could respond, a gun went off.

"Ah, fuck!" he screamed. I snapped my head in the direction of Los who was holding his smoking gun.

"That's a warning shot, bitch. Keep being a smart ass and the next one is a headshot," he snapped. The rest of the guys sat there.

"Aye, I probably received about the same amount as Malachi did. I don't have it on me, but I can bring that shit to you tomorrow. I want no parts in being on your bad side," another nigga named Bruno chimed in. The other two nodded in agreement as Sly winced in pain from the graze in his arm.

"For the next month, y'all are only getting fifty percent of your cut," I said.

"What? I just said I had the money I took," Bruno stood to his feet.

"Nigga I don't give a damn. I'm taking back what's

mine and then I'm charging y'all asses for making me have to even address this dumb ass shit. This is me being nice because I would much rather be elsewhere than waiting for y'all to stop being bitches and be honest," I let them know. "Get the fuck out."

They all stood to their feet and shuffled out of the warehouse. The moment they left, I began questioning if remaining in this business was the right thing to do. Before Gabby and Infinity came into my life, I wouldn't have let these niggas walk out.

"You good?" Los questioned.

"Yeah, why, what's up?"

"Because your head seems elsewhere. You let these niggas walk, which is surprising to me."

"Shit, me too," I told him honestly. "I have a feeling that nigga Sly is going to be a problem though."

"You thinking the exact same thing I am. He ain't gonna last. I'm gonna put one of the hittas on his ass. He's too cocky and that's the last thing we need." I nodded in agreement before we both stood up, dapped each other up, and headed out of the warehouse. The ride back to Infinity's was smooth. I was glad there was no traffic. I pulled up to her house and sat there for a moment, reflecting on my life.

So much had changed in such a short amount of time. Before my daughter, all I cared about was getting up and getting to the money. Ever since she came into my life, I found myself questioning when I was getting out of the game. I never wanted my daughter to see this side of my life. I never wanted the game to take me from my daughter. At that moment, I realized it was time for me to start thinking of and making the necessary changes to get my ass out of the game before it was too late. I sighed as I killed the engine and headed inside to crawl up under my girl. As I walked into her bedroom, I stripped down to my boxers and headed to take a quick shower before climbing into the bed with her. Within twenty minutes, I was sliding into bed with her, and it took me no time before I fell into a deep sleep.

Chapter Twenty - Two

Infinity Morrison

I groaned as I heard my alarm going off. I was kicking myself in the ass for not shutting it off before I went to bed. I had to pry Ace's around from around me to reach my phone on the nightstand. I quickly silenced it and stood to walk to the bathroom. The moment I sat on the toilet, the emotions from last night rushed me again. I took a few deep breaths because I didn't want to end up crying again. I wiped myself, flushed the toilet, and began handling my hygiene.

Walking out of the bathroom, I saw that Ace was still asleep. I had no idea what time he returned last night, but I would be lying if I said I didn't enjoy waking up to him. I walked back over to my side of the bed and climbed back in the bed. He shifted so that his head was on my lap. I could hear the light snores as I smiled and rubbed his head. I leaned against the headboard and thought about where I was in life. Every dream I had set out for myself, I had accomplished. The only thing missing was a child of my own. I looked down at Ace again and silently thanked God for him. Everything between us was still fresh, but the way he was there for me was something I would forever be grateful for.

I grabbed my phone off the nightstand and opened the app to my GYN office. I put in a request to make an appointment. Even if Ace and I didn't make it, for myself, I had to know if what that doctor told me years ago was indeed true. If I still had the opportunity to actually have children of my own, I would do whatever I had to, even if it meant IVF. Once I submitted the request for my appointment, I opened my Facebook app and went to the inbox for my business page. I clicked on Jermaine's page. I scrolled a little to see if I could see anything, yet it was nothing but random memes he shared. I noticed him tagged in a picture of his girlfriend and smiled at the little girl in the picture. She was adorable and looked exactly like her father. I swallowed the lump that formed in my throat as I thought about my son. I took a deep breath and tapped on the icon to send him a message.

My hands shook a little as I began to type.

Me (5:54 a.m.) – Give me a call when you get a moment. You can call me through Facebook.

I sent the message, locked my phone and I leaned my head back and closed my eyes.

I hadn't realized that I had fallen asleep until I felt soft kisses being placed along my face. Peeking out of one eye, my eyes landed on Ace who was smirking.

"Morning," I greeted.

"Morning, beautiful. You look hella uncomfortable," he chuckled.

I rotated my neck to loosen it up before I stretched.

"A little. I hadn't even realized I had fallen asleep."

"What time did you get up?"

"I forgot to shut my alarm off, so I was up at five-thirty."

"How are you feeling?"

I shrugged. "I'll be okay."

"Do you want to go out for breakfast?" he offered.

"N-. Actually, sure."

"Where do you want to go?"

"Surprise me," I smirked as I stretched and threw the blanket back to climb out of bed. The moment I stood, Ace slapped me on the ass. I chuckled and headed to the bathroom to relieve my bladder again. Once I was done, I handled my hygiene. We both got dressed in silence, but it wasn't long before my vibrating phone broke the silence. Scooping it up, I saw it was my doctor's office.

"Hello."

"Hi, this is Sabrina and I'm calling from Dr. Denson's office. Can I speak to Infinity, please?"

"This is she."

"Hi, Infinity. We received your request for an appointment and wanted to see what day and time worked for you to come in."

"Any time and any day, honestly," I told her.

"We have an opening tomorrow at one."

"That's fine."

"Great. I will book you for that slot and we will see you then."

"Thank you."

I ended the call and took a deep breath. I was nervous about the appointment, but I would go in with an open mind.

"Everything okay?"

I nodded and told him about the call.

"Do you want me to go with you?"

"No, it's okay."

"Make sure you let me know how it works out," he said. I nodded and we both finished getting dressed. Within thirty minutes, I was locking up the door and heading to the car. I couldn't lie, after running into Jermaine yesterday, I was filled with anxiety about being outside today, but one thing I refused to do was allow him to keep me holed in the house.

"You like T's?"

"Yeah, they're good."

The car became silent between us again and I stared out the window.

"Aye," Ace spoke, breaking the silence. "Whatever it is that is bothering you, let it go. Everything will work out the way that it's supposed to. One thing about that nigga yesterday, he clearly doesn't know shit about you."

I offered a small smile and appreciated Ace for trying to take my mind off what Jermaine said, but it was easier said than done. I silently prayed for a miracle tomorrow at my appointment. I meant what I said regarding I wouldn't care what ropes I would have to climb over to get a child, I would have my own as long as the doctor and God said it was possible.

In less than ten minutes, we pulled into the parking lot of T's. Ace killed the engine and we both climbed out. He came around the car and grabbed my hand, holding it tightly as we walked inside. The small gesture brought me a sense of safety and peace. The hostess greeted us and we were quickly seated. It wasn't long before the waitress returned to take our drink orders. As we waited, I pulled out my phone to check the cameras at the center. I trusted Jas and Mel with my life, so I knew they were holding things down in my absence. I made a mental note to fill them in on what happened. I felt someone staring at me. Looking up, I saw Ace damn near burning a hole in my face.

"You okay?" I questioned.

"Yeah, I just want to make sure that you're okay."

I couldn't help the smile that broke across my face. It felt good to have someone who openly cared about my feelings. Sometimes, the simple, '*are you okay?*' means the world.

"Yeah," I sighed. "I'm anxious for tomorrow though."

"Everything will work out in your favor. We are going to remain positive. Don't stress about it," he stated as he rubbed my hand. I smirked but didn't say anything as the waitress returned with our drinks and took our food orders. Once she was gone, Ace and I made small talk.

An hour later, we walked out of the restaurant hand in hand. Ace held the car door open for me as I climbed in.

"Is there anything else you wanna do today?" he asked.

I shrugged. "You have something you need to do?"

"I gotta go check on a few things sometime today, but nothing urgent," he responded as he pulled out his phone. Before I could say anything else, he sighed heavily.

"What's wrong?"

He shook his head, put the car into gear, and pulled off without responding. I stared at him for a little while to see if he would respond, and when he turned up the music, I figured he wasn't. I turned and watched the city pass me by. Before I knew it, we were pulling up to my house. I noticed he stopped but didn't put the car in park. He remained staring out the driver's side window. I could tell whatever was on his phone, had him upset. I waited a few seconds for him to say something, but he didn't say anything. Rather than break the silence, I climbed out of the car and made my way toward my door. I glanced back at the car before entering and noticed he was looking at me. I offered a small smile but got nothing in return. I headed inside and my mind began running a million miles a minute. I didn't know what had happened that fast to cause the turn in his mood, and I didn't want to dwell on it.

I sighed, locked the door behind me, and headed to my room to take a nap. Just as I stripped down to climb into bed, my phone began ringing. Based on the tone, I knew it was coming from Facebook Messenger. Looking at the screen, I took a deep breath when I saw it was Jermaine calling. I knew I had to get this done and over with though, so I went ahead and answered.

"Hello?"

"What's good? Never thought I would see a message from you telling you to call," he stated right off the back. I rolled my eyes.

"Never thought I would be telling you to call me, but you've been seeming to have something to get off of your chest, so here's your chance."

"What?"

"I'm saying, you messaged me about my center asking to get up and chill and then you felt the need to try and embarrass me in public. Now, I'm giving you the opportunity you so desperately seem to want," I stated.

He chuckled. "I honestly was just tryna see if you were straight. You up and dipped on me all those years ago. I always told you I wanted you to have my child and you always said no, but now your ass has a baby by another nigga."

I felt my body warm up.

"Let's get something straight," I cut him off before he could say anything. "You killed any chance of us having a child together when I found out you were fuckin' bitches raw and not giving a whole fuck about me and my health. You have a child with someone else, so there is no need for me to even entertain that shit anymore. For your information though, you do have a son who unfortunately didn't make it. When I left your ass, I was pregnant. I carried my son until almost six months before I suffered a miscarriage at twenty-two weeks pregnant. I had an emergency c-section, which left me unable to even bear children." I didn't realize I was crying until I felt my cheek become moist.

"What? Why did you never tell me?"

"Why would I? You didn't give a shit about me, and you made that clear as day. I wasn't about to stress another damn minute about your ass. It's just sad that after all the years we spent together, you still don't know shit about me. All I've ever wanted was to be a fuckin' mother, but I was deprived of that opportunity. You have a child. You know what it's like to be a parent. I'll never fuckin' get that."

"A'ight, man. Chill," he said.

"No, fuck you! I thought I wanted to hear what you had to say, but you just proved that I was cool with never speaking to you again."

He sighed and the phone went silent. Just as I was about to hang up, he broke the silence.

"Where is he? Is he buried anywhere?"

"No, he was cremated. You can continue on as if you never knew about him," I told him.

"That'll never happen, Infinity. Listen, for real, I'm sorry you had to go through that alone. That shit will never sit right with me. All bullshit aside, I'm sorry for the shit I've done to you. As the father of a daughter, I never want my daughter to deal with any of the shit I've done to you. I would body a nigga for doing that shit to mine."

I couldn't lie, I was speechless. I never thought I would hear an apology from Jermaine, and I gave up on ever getting one. Finally getting one from him, did something to me.

"I appreciate that. After this, I would appreciate you no longer reaching out to me. If you see me on the street, pretend you don't know me. It's the best for me." I ended the call and immediately blocked him. I took a few deep breaths and wiped my face. I slid down in bed and pulled the covers up to my neck. Looking at my nightstand, my eyes landed on my son's urn.

"I love you, Bentley."

I made sure to put my phone on loud just in case Ace had text or called me. Part of me wanted to reach out, but I was sure once he was done doing whatever he was doing, he would call. Until then, I hoped for the best for him.

Chapter Twenty - Three

Deandre 'Ace' Lemetti

I was seething, and seeing red. I hated to leave Infinity abruptly, but I feared if I said something to her, it would come out wrong and she would take it as I was snapping at her and that wasn't the case at all. Replaying the message that I read through my mind, I pressed on the gas harder as I sped toward my mother's house.

Turning onto her street, damn near on two wheels, I smashed on the brakes, leaving tire treads outside of my mother's house. I barely put the car into park before I jumped out and rushed into the house. Slamming the door behind me, I knew she would chew my head off, but right now, I didn't care.

"Slam something else and I'm slamming you," my mother told me, handing me the manilla envelope. I didn't bother to say anything as I snatched the envelope and damn near tore it open. Scanning over the document, I had to run my tongue over my teeth and count to ten. My eye began twitching and I could feel my trigger finger itching. Aaliyah was taking me to court for primary custody of Gabby. "Deandre," my mother called out to me. I didn't respond verbally, but I looked at her. "I don't know what you're feeling, but I know that look in your eye. All I'm going to say is to be smart. Don't react off impulse because there is no telling what she has told or will tell them about you."

I closed my eyes and took a deep breath. A range of emotions was flowing through my body. Ashton Kutcher had to be ready to jump out at me. He had to be. There was no way my life was being tossed into shambles because a bitch decided she wants to play mother after being gone for a year.

"I'm just gonna call my lawyer. It's taking everything in me to not call her and give her a piece of my mind," I told my mother.

"I know, and that's probably what she's expecting, but don't give in to her. You keep doing what you have to do for Gabby. If you can, keep all communication with her through text. Unfortunately, you might have to let her see Gabby."

"What?" I snapped.

"If she shows proof that she's been trying to see the child and you're not allowing her to, it could backfire."

"I ain't tryna hear all that," I waved her off. "I have custody of her. The mother section of her birth certificate is blank, so as far as I'm concerned, she doesn't have a mother," I told her honestly.

"Run it by your lawyer and see what he says. If he says you don't have to let her around, then so be it. I just want you to move smart and not do anything that'll come back to bite you in the ass."

I continued to scan over the document in my hand telling me she was trying to take my baby from me. I blew out a deep breath and walked away from my mom.

"Is she here?" I asked.

"No, I took her to daycare this morning. She wasn't about to drive me nuts on my day off," she chuckled. I shook my head and headed toward my old room. Once inside, I sat on the bed and closed my eyes to calm myself. A few minutes later, I pulled out my phone, scrolled to my lawyer's name and tapped on it.

"Dre, to what do I owe this call?" he answered on the first ring.

"Are you in the office?"

"I'll be there in about five minutes. Everything good?"

"For the most part. I'll meet you there."

"Sounds good."

We ended the call as I went into my stash and pulled a few stacks to throw him some extra. I didn't know how much work he was going to have to do for this to work in my favor, but to keep my baby with me, I would pay him whatever.

"Ma, I'm out," I yelled.

"Are you picking up Gabby?" she questioned.

"Yeah."

"Okay. I love you, son."

"Love you too, old lady."

I jumped in my ride, cranked it up, and rushed downtown to my lawyer's office. I needed him to tell me some good news that would prevent me from tracking Aaliyah's bitch ass down and laying hands on her for trying to play with me. Thankfully, traffic was light, so I was able to reach his office within twelve minutes flat. I nodded at the security guard and headed to the elevator. I pulled out my phone as I rode the elevator to Trevor's twelfth-floor office, but it didn't take me long to reach his floor since nobody else got on. I gave his secretary a head nod as I made my way into his office without waiting for them to let him know I was there.

"Dre, what's going on?" he questioned when I closed the door.

"My BM is trying to take me to court for my daughter," I blurted out. "I need to know what to expect and if I have to give her access to my child before all of this is said and done." I plopped down in the seat across from him.

"Well, when we did the custody thing, it was so that you have full, sole, and physical custody with placement. To answer your question, no, you do not have to give access to the child to her unless a judge throws out your custody agreement and gives her joint custody," he explained.

"Is there any way that she can be granted full custody?" The thought of losing my baby girl gave me a bad taste in my mouth.

194

"If she can prove you're unfit and a danger to your daughter. It's not going to be a good look that she completely went MIA for a year. You have the letter that she left you with your daughter on your porch, so that'll help you," Trevor explained. I feel like I was able to breathe a little easier now that he made things clear for me.

"If she reaches out to me, do I have to respond?"

"Are you able to talk to her calmly?" he retorted.

"No. Honestly, every time I see or think about her, it makes my blood boil. I can understand needing to get your life together, and while she apparently did that *after*, she didn't leave my daughter for that reason."

"I'll put it like this. You don't have to communicate with her because again, you're the custodial parent. However, I guess it'll look better if you try. I'm not saying that you have to reach out to her, but if she reaches out to you, it will look better if you respond."

I sighed heavily because I truly wanted nothing to do with Aaliyah. Not even a little bit. I didn't want to try with her, or anything. I simply wanted her to forget both Gabby and I existed and go back to whatever she was doing before.

"A'ight. Well, I was served today for a custody battle, so you may want to get geared up for that," I told him as I tossed ten stacks on his desk. He quickly pushed the money back in my direction.

"You know I don't need that."

"I didn't say you did. I just know sometimes custody battles can get messy, so I wanted to throw you something extra just in case. Let me know what I need to do for this shit," I stated as I stood to leave.

"I got you."

While I was not fully in the clear, I did feel better after discussing my concerns with Trevor. I pulled my phone out of my back pocket and saw a missed call and text from Infinity. I didn't bother opening the message, and instead returned her call.

The call rolled over to voicemail. I hung up and dialed her number again. She didn't answer the second time, so I went to the text thread, and read her message.

Wifey (2:21 PM): *Not sure what happened, but I hope everything is okay. Xoxo.*

Me (3:02 PM): *My bad. I tried to call you back a few times, but I'm assuming you're sleeping. Give me a call when you see this.*

I thought about going back by her house but decided to check on the shit I needed to handle before I had to pick up Gabby. I pushed the bullshit with Aaliyah to the back of my mind as I shot Los a message letting him know I was about to pull up on him. I had to run some shit by him. I knew one thing was for sure. Aaliyah was gonna play dirty, and I needed to clean my money and quickly.

Chapter Twenty - Four
Infinity Morrison

The following morning, I tried to keep myself busy at work and tried not to think about the upcoming doctor's appointment. I had been texting Ace all morning about how nervous I was, and he was doing his best to keep me calm too. I checked my watch and saw that it was time to start preparing the trays for lunch, and I would be heading out once that was done. The kitchen aid had lunch finished, so I loaded up the trays and headed to the toddler rooms. I quickly dispersed the trays and returned the carts to the kitchen. I shot Jas and Mel a text letting them know I would be stepping out for about an hour. Jas and Mel both had access to the cameras, and I knew with both of their lunch breaks coming up, they would both man the front while I was gone.

It was ten minutes to one when I pulled up to my doctor's office. I sat and took a few deep breaths. I closed my eyes and counted to ten. A knock at my window damn near had me pissing on myself. I looked in the direction of the knock and my heart skipped a beat when I saw Ace standing there. I smiled softly before killing the engine and stepping out.

"Hey," I greeted as I pecked his lips softly. "What are you doing here?"

"Supporting you. You're too nervous to be here alone, in my opinion."

I blushed and dropped my head.

"Thank you," I said just above a whisper. I had no idea what this appointment would entail, but I would be lying if I said my nerves weren't all over the place. Hand in hand, we walked across the parking lot and into the doctor's office.

"Hi. How can I help you?" the receptionist greeted me.

"Hi, I have a one o'clock appointment with Dr. Denson."

"What's your name and date of birth?"

"Infinity Morrison. April 12th, 1992." She clicked around on her screen before asking me to verify my address, and phone number, and provide an insurance card. When she gave me my copay amount, Ace wasted no time digging into his pocket. The receptionist looked from me to Ace before taking his card from him. Once I was fully checked in, she told me to have a seat.

When we sat down, my leg instantly started bouncing out of habit.

"Chill, Ma. Everything will be good." Ace kissed the side of my face for good measure, and while I tried to calm myself, nothing was working.

"Infinity," I heard my name called.

"Do you need me to come back?"

"N-no. I think I'll be good," I told him, completely unsure of myself.

"If you need me, I'm here." I gave him a small smile before I walked off to where the medical assistant was waiting to check me in. My vitals, weight and height were taken, and I was put in a room where I was told the doctor would be in to see me.

Sitting in that room by myself, I was left alone to my thoughts, which was dangerous. Every negative thought that could have run through my mind, did. Thankfully, it didn't take long for Dr. Denson to come in.

"Hi, Infinity. How are you?"

"I'm okay. How are you?"

"Can't complain. What brings you in today?"

I sighed. "Well as you know, I suffered a late-term miscarriage a few years ago and I was told that due to the emergency c-section, I wouldn't be able to have children because of how damaged my scar tissue was. I never looked into it to see if it was truly damaged and if my chances of having my own child were really as low as they stated," I told her with tears welling in my eyes.

"Are you considering having a baby?" she questioned.

"I never considered it because I was told I couldn't have them, but I've longed for a chance to be a mother ever since I was pregnant with my son. I left my son's dad before I found out I was pregnant, and after losing my son, I focused on me. I'm now in a better position for myself and have met an amazing man."

"Is he trying to force this on you?" she questioned. I twisted my face. I knew she meant well, but I wasn't a fan of her question.

"What? No!" I sighed. "He has a daughter of his own." I looked up at the ceiling to try and keep my tears at bay. "Listen, Dr. Denson. I have worked in a childcare facility since I was sixteen. I recently opened my own center. Deep down, I've always wondered what it would be like to be a mother. I was ripped of that chance by losing my son. I love these children that walk through my center, and I want the opportunity to experience the only kind of love that children give their parents. Yes, the new man in my life is the one who encouraged me to come and see you to find out what my chances truly are with being able to conceive a baby. He gave that encouragement based on hearing my hurt of losing my son and the desire to actually have my own child."

"I understand. Well, what I can do is send you over to radiology and have them perform an ultrasound. Once I get those results back, I'll review them to check your scar tissue and we can go from there. Also, I'll send you to get some bloodwork. If everything indeed does check out, we can make sure you're healthy enough to go through pregnancy. Sometimes, it's an undiagnosed medical condition that can cause a miscarriage, or unfortunately, they just happen. Either way, we should know when the labs and ultrasound comes back," she explained.

"Okay, sounds good."

"Give me a few minutes to get the referral for ultrasound and the lab slips together. When would you like me to schedule the ultrasound?"

"Any day works."

"Okay. I'll be right back." Within ten minutes, there was a knock at the door before she peeked in. "Radiology has an appointment available in fifteen minutes due to a cancellation. Can you go now?"

"Yes," I exclaimed as I hopped off the table.

"Okay. The lab slip for bloodwork will be at the front desk when you check out. I should have the results by tomorrow, so schedule a follow-up for the day after for us to go over them," she said.

"Will do."

I was excited they were able to get me in so soon. I damn near ran to the desk to check out and walk across the street to the radiology department. During the walk, I explained to Ace what the doctor had told me. As always, he spoke positivity into me. One thing was for sure, I was glad his baby's mother fumbled him because he truly was the breath of fresh air I needed in my life.

*****

Two Days Later…

I sat on the exam bed in the doctor's office twiddling my thumbs as I waited for Dr. Denson to come in. These last forty-eight hours seemed to be the longest forty-eight hours ever. Ace had to handle something, so he wasn't able to attend the appointment with me. However, he made sure to call me before I walked in the door to keep my nerves at ease. The light knock at the door caused me to jump.

"Come in," I called.

"Hi, Infinity. Sorry, it took me so long. I had to print out the lab results and of course, the printer ran out of paper in the middle of printing," she chuckled. "How are you?"

"Anxious," I told her honestly.

"Understandable. Alright, so the ultrasound did reveal damaged scar tissue. I'm not sure why they cut it the way they did, but it could have been neater." I swallowed hard and dropped my head. I felt the lump forming in my throat and I wanted to let out the deepest sob I could from the pit of my soul. "However," she continued. "It's not damaged where it's dangerous to carry a baby to term. From the ultrasound, it still looks thick enough to where you can successfully carry a baby. Your tubes are still intact, also the uterus looks good and is functioning well. I will say that because of the damage to your scar tissue, that if you should get pregnant, I would want you to take it easy. You probably won't have to do bed rest, but I would keep it all work to light duty."

I could not stop the tears that fell even if I tried. I sobbed and I sobbed hard, snot dripping and all. I jumped off the table and hugged her tightly. My prayers had been answered. There was a light at the end of the tunnel for me.

"Thank you, Dr. Denson. Thank you so much."

"You don't have to thank me," she said. I could hear her getting choked up. "I couldn't imagine being in your position, so young, and being told you'll never be able to do something almost every woman desires to do. Whenever it does happen, I will be right here to get you through it," she assured me. I finally let her go and wiped my face. I closed my eyes, thanking God and my son. I knew this was nobody but Bentley.

I wrapped up my appointment with Dr. Denson and checked out of my appointment. The moment I stepped off the elevator, I dialed Ace's number. I wanted nothing more than to share the news with him. My call rolled over to voicemail. I tried to call him again but was met with the same result. I tried a third time and received the same response. I decided to text him and tell him to call me when he could. I took a moment and sat in my car to cry more. I couldn't believe for years I believed my chances of becoming a mom were gone when in reality, they weren't. I checked my phone for a response from Ace, but my lock screen was empty. I shifted my car into gear and headed back to work, this time with a wide and genuine smile.

Chapter Twenty - Five

Aaliyah Murphy

I sighed as I sat at the table in the lunchroom and checked my phone. I saw I had an email from my lawyer that let me know Ace was successfully served with the custody papers. Truthfully, I didn't want to go through court. I had hoped that Ace would work with me, but the more he refused, the more my hand was forced. I couldn't lie, though. I was nervous as hell going up against him in court. It was no secret that Ace's money was longer than mine, and I knew he would go to no end to keep Gabby. I knew it wasn't a good look that I had left her on his porch the way I did. I had spoken to my lawyer about it and she told me the argument would be that I wasn't mentally stable enough to raise a child, therefore, I did the best thing I could have, which was leave her with her father.

Every day I kicked myself in the ass for how I handled things, but I truly had changed, and I wanted to right my wrongs. Gabby wouldn't remember being left on Ace's porch, but Ace would never forget it and I was sure he wouldn't let me forget it either.

I went to social media and checked Deanna's page for any updated pictures of Gabby, but she hadn't posted any. I stared at the last one she posted two weeks prior and smiled. My baby girl was truly beautiful, and I had to give it to Ace, he had done a great job with her so far. She was happy, healthy, and thriving based on the videos I had seen Deanna post of her.

Just as I was about to stop scrolling my Facebook timeline, a sponsored post from a daycare center popped up. *To Infinity and Beyond Learning Center.* It was the woman standing outside of the center that caught my attention. It was Ace's friend. I quickly clicked on the page and began scrolling. I could see she was advertising both jobs as she was hiring, and open spots for kids. I went to the pictures on the center's page and my heart skipped a beat when I saw my Gabby. I scrolled through all of their pictures and videos, and I had to give it to her, her center looked amazing. The curriculum she showed as well as the videos of the children showcasing what they learned brought a smile to my face. I was glad my daughter would be getting that type of education.

I then wondered if this was how she and Ace met. I went back to the center's main page and read the *About* section. Once I was done, I then searched for the name Infinity, and ironically, Infinity Janae was the first page that popped up. I scrolled her page and had to admit, she was a beautiful woman. Part of me wanted to friend request her, but I'm sure the last interaction we had was enough for her to look at me sideways.

I closed out of my Facebook app and finally opened my lunch to eat before my break was over. My mind went back to the custody case I opened. I was tempted to try and reach out to Ace to work this out between us, but I was sure he had my number blocked and wouldn't hesitate to call the cops if I showed up at his house. I decided after work, I would write him a letter and drop it in his mailbox, asking him to rethink this keeping me from Gabby situation before the courts got involved, to see if maybe he would change his mind. If he didn't, then I would have no choice but to go ahead and let the court handle it. Either way; I was only looking for one outcome and that was to finally get the chance to be a mom to my daughter. That's it and that's all.

Holding the Key to a Hustla's Heart

Chapter Twenty - Six

Deandre 'Ace' Lemetti

I wrapped up business with Los just before eleven at night. This had taken longer than anticipated, but I had gotten everything done that needed to be done. My lawyer had located a few businesses that seemed to either be struggling financially or that were selling. By the end of the weekend, I would either be a full or part owner in at least three businesses and I could start washing my funds. I was able to breathe a little easier because I wasn't sure if Aaliyah would try and bring my illegal dealings into this battle, but just in case, I could now back it up. Thankfully, the owners were even willing to backdate at least a year for me too. One thing was for sure, money talked.

I made it to my car and grabbed my phone from the cupholder. I sighed at all the missed calls and texts. This was the downside to business. I always had to remain focused because, in this line of work, distractions are how niggas either got killed, robbed, or locked up. I started with the texts and saw that my mother was cursing me out. She ended by letting me know Infinity picked up Gabby because my mother was called into work. I decided to call her back tomorrow because if I called her tonight, she would surely burst an eardrum with her yelling. I did shoot her a text telling her I loved her and to have a good night at work. I smirked when I saw the bubbles immediately pop up on the screen, letting me know she was responding.

I then went over to Infinity's messages. There were a few telling me to call her, a few telling me she was concerned, and the final one of a picture of Gabby sleeping and her telling me she had her at her place. I hearted the picture and dropped the phone back down. I washed my hands over my face before pulling away from the spot. I sparked up the blunt I rolled earlier as I made my way to Infinity's place. The streets were empty on this Wednesday night, so it didn't take me long to get there.

I sat in the lot and finished my blunt before killing the engine and walking to the door. I saw the living room light on, so I figured she was sitting there, so I knocked lightly and stood to the side. A few seconds later, I heard the locks turning.

"Hey, I'm glad you're okay," she said as she let me in.

"Sorry about that. I had left my phone in the car and locked in to handle the business I needed to handle," I explained, closing and locking the door behind me.

"I figured that when I talked to your mom. She said this is typically what happens when you're working," she chuckled.

"Did you eat?"

"Nah. I'm starving too." I sat on the couch, kicked my shoes off, and grabbed her hand to pull her into my lap before I started planting kisses along her jawline. "You cooked?"

"Yeah."

"You save me some?" Her breathing was becoming labored as I ran my hand up and down her thigh and continued planting kisses on her cheek.

"Y-yes." I planted one more kiss and chuckled as she had her eyes closed.

"Let me stop." Her eyes popped open, and she mushed me before standing up. "How was your appointment?" I asked, sitting at the table as she unwrapped the plate and placed it in the microwave.

She turned around and smiled hard at me. "She said my scar tissue is damaged, but not severe enough to where I can't carry to term. My lab work checked out, too. So I just haven't gotten pregnant because I hadn't had sex," she laughed. "The only thing she said is to just take it easy whenever I do become pregnant. She said that I should keep all work to light duty, but she doesn't see why I wouldn't be able to conceive or carry."

"That's what's up, mama. I'm glad you finally got the right information."

"Me too. I can't lie, deep down that always made me insecure. I felt like less of a woman because I couldn't do the one thing women are supposed to do naturally."

"Aye," I called to get her attention. "Don't say no shit like that. Whether you were able to do it naturally or with a little medical help, you're still one hundred percent woman. You're no less than the next."

She gave a small smile as the microwave went off. She pulled the food out, grabbed a fork, and slid the plate over to me. I wasted no time diving into the piping hot lasagna as she placed a tall glass of juice in front of me. She sat across from me and watched me eat with a small smirk on her face.

"Why you looking at me like that?"

She shrugged. "I'm honestly wondering how I got so lucky to come across someone like you. How the hell have you remained on the market as long as you have?"

"I'm selective with who I give my real time. I can fuck any bitch, but not just anyone gets Deandre. Any and everyone can get Ace."

"You never wanted to settle down?" she questioned.

"Of course, I did, but not just with anyone. At one point, I thought it would be with Aaliyah, but you see how that turned out. After that, it just became about getting money and being successful, to me. When Gabby came into my life, it was about her. And then you came." I winked at her and watched as she blushed. "Clearly, the man above knew what he was doing when he kept both of us on the market and had us crossing paths."

She didn't respond as I finished eating. Once I was done, I washed my plate and cup before grabbing her hand and heading to the bedroom. She climbed into bed while I grabbed clothes and took a quick shower and handled my hygiene. When I came out, I found Gabby and Infinity sleeping. I grabbed my phone and took a quick picture before I climbed into bed with them. I hadn't realized how tired I was until I found myself dozing off a short time later.

*****

A Few Weeks Later...

I pulled up to Infinity's center shortly after noon. I figured by now the walkthrough would be done. She had been stressing badly about the first inspection from the state, although I knew she would be fine because her center was legit. I grabbed the bag of food from the Spanish restaurant she loved, the bouquet of roses, and the vanilla chai she drank regardless of the weather outside. Spring was breaking through, Infinity's birthday was coming up, as well as this mediation bullshit with Aaliyah. She had been quiet as far as I knew, but I knew it wouldn't be long before she tried some bullshit, so I stayed on alert for her.

I reached the door and rang the bell. When Infinity came to the lobby, a huge smile graced her face as she saw me standing there. She unlocked the door and held it open for me.

"Hey, what are you doing here?" she questioned as she grabbed the bag from my hand.

"I wanted to bring you lunch and a little pick me up. How did the inspection go?"

213

"Perfect! We passed and thankfully won't have to see them for another year," she said, letting out a deep breath.

"I told you shit would be good. You stressed about it for nothing." I followed her into her office.

"I know, I know. I just couldn't help it. I'm glad it's over. What did you bring?"

"Yellow rice and beef with extra sauce on the rice and a vanilla chai, which is a fucked-up combination, but it's your stomach, not mine," I joked as I placed her drink down. She flipped me off, grabbed the roses, sniffed them, and replaced a dead bouquet that she had in the vase in the window.

"Thank you for this."

"No need to thank me. I do have a question for you though."

"Uh oh. What's up?"

"How much time can you take off of work?"

She paused mid-way through, putting her food in her mouth. She set the spoon down and sat back in her seat with a raised eyebrow.

"Technically, I can take as much time as I need. Why?"

"Can you take off the week of your birthday for me?"

She cocked her head to the side.

"Why?"

"Can you just do what I asked, please? Shit. Stop asking so many questions. All you have to do is take the time off and I'll handle the rest for us."

"Fine." She threw her hands up in the air. "Besides taking the time off of work, is there anything else I need to do to prepare before then?" I could tell she was being sarcastic, so I shook my head and laughed.

"Just trust me, mama. I'm gonna let you get back to your day. I just wanted to stop in to check on you and bring you something to eat." I walked around and leaned down to plant a kiss on her lips. "Don't work too hard, a'ight?" She nodded before puckering up for another kiss. "Love you, beautiful."

She paused and looked at me and I didn't miss the tears welling in her eyes.

"Stop being emotional, girl," I chuckled as I wiped her eyes. "I say what I mean and mean what I say. If you ain't ready, then that's cool, but I'm not going to hide my love for you." I kissed her lips again and then her forehead. She still sat there stuck. "Call me if you need me."

I grabbed my keys off her desk and headed out. Even without Infinity saying anything, I knew she loved me. Her actions showed it; and to me, actions spoke louder than words.

Chapter Twenty - Seven

Infinity Morrison

I sat at my desk stuck for a few minutes. Did I love Ace? Absolutely, but I expected to be the first one to say it to him. I didn't doubt he loved me, but he surprised me by saying it and I felt like an idiot sitting here looking like a damn bump on a log. I dug my phone out of my desk and quickly dialed his number.

"Missing me already?" he answered on the second ring.

"I love you more," I spat. The phone became silent, so I had to check the screen to make sure the call hadn't dropped.

"I know. Get back to work."

"Okay."

We ended the call, and I sat there staring at the wall. My vibrating phone broke my silence. Glancing at the screen, I couldn't stop the smile that graced my face.

"Look who decided to re-muthafuckin'-surface," I answered.

217

"I know, bitch! I miss my best friend so fuckin' much. School and work are whooping my ass. I finally have time for the outside world with spring break," Dani shouted. Dani was working on her master's degree and outside of quick check-in texts, it had been months since I had a serious conversation with her or even seen her. "We have to catch up."

"We definitely do!"

"How's the center?"

"It's great! We had our first inspection today, and passed with flying colors, so that's a weight off my shoulders. You know I freak out over the smallest shit, so I was on edge the whole time until they got there, and while they were here."

"That's always been you, Fin," she chuckled. "Let me know when you're free so we can catch up."

"I'm out of the center usually by six and off weekends. I kind of have a man now though."

"Bitch, what? How does someone kind of have a man?"

"Well, I have one," I responded, laughing at her antics.

"You know what, fuck waiting. Six-thirty tonight, meet me at 148 for drinks and wings! I feel like I don't even know you anymore."

"Aww, now you know it's nothing like that, Dani. Nobody can replace you."

"Tell me anything."

I rolled my eyes and smiled. Dani could be so damn dramatic, but I loved her and all her extraness.

"I'll meet you there, boo."

"Okay, cool. Love you."

"Love you more."

We ended the call, and I finished my lunch as I shot Ace a text letting him know my after-work plans. I blushed at the thought of reporting my whereabouts to anyone.

"What got you blushing?" Jas asked stepping into my office.

"Just thinking," I told her as I continued to eat. Jas didn't push the issue as she pulled out her lunch and began to eat with me. We made small talk during her break and then she headed back to her room. The rest of the day was smooth and thankfully all the parents were on time, including Ace. He told me to let him know when I was done kickin' it with Dani. Once the center was empty and I did my room-to-room walkthrough, I locked up and headed out. I pulled up five minutes after the time Dani gave me, but I spotted her car and knew she was waiting for me inside. I tucked my purse away, grabbed my wallet and phone, and headed inside. I spotted Dani sitting at the table with a drink. I made my way over to her and she jumped up, squealing, and met me.

"Oh, my fuckin' God! I've missed you!"

"I've missed you too, Dee. Never the fuck again will we go this damn long without seeing each other," I told her as we both sat at the table. Once we did, the bartender came over to us to take my drink and wing order.

"For real! Last semester of school and I'm fuckin' done," she exclaimed.

"I'm proud of you, boo."

"I appreciate you, sis. Now tell me, what's new with you with your *I might have a man* ass."

I laughed and thanked the bartender for bringing me the drink. Before I responded, I took a sip of my drink.

"He's one of the parents at my center," I explained.

"Wait, what?"

I chuckled and filled her in on my situation with Ace. I was smiling so damn hard, my cheeks were aching.

"Whaaaat!" she exclaimed. I couldn't help but laugh. "Nah, all jokes aside, I'm happy for you. He seems to make you happy, and if anyone deserves happiness, it's you."

"Thank you. Oh wait, I didn't tell you. I saw Jermaine."

Dani began coughing as she choked on her drink.

"What? When? Where the fuck he come from?" I rolled my eyes as I replayed the situation at Chuck E. Cheese and then downed my drink. Dani started going off about how much of a bitch ass nigga Jermaine was. I couldn't help but laugh as the bartender dropped the wing basket on the table. We thanked her, requested a refill for our drinks, and began digging into our food. "Besides all that bullshit, how have you been?"

"I'm good," I told her honestly. "I recently found out some good news."

"What, you pregnant?"

"Bitch, if I was pregnant, would I be sitting here throwing

back drinks with you, simple?" I questioned.

"Shit, if I found out I was, I would be so surprised that I might have a drink or two. Who the fuck knows?"

I couldn't help but laugh and shake my head. I missed my girl, and I didn't realize how much I did until I was in her presence. I proceeded to fill her in on my doctor's appointment and she immediately stopped eating and her mouth hung open.

"Are you serious?" I smiled hard and nodded my head. "Bitch, that's amazing! Let me stake claim as godmother because I know my godchild is coming before the end of the damn year! Matter of fact, let me see a picture of your nigga. Your ass might be getting pregnant tonight."

"Hell naw! My birthday is in two weeks, I need to be able to turn up then. I think he's planning on taking me out somewhere because he asked me to take the week off from work."

"I'm gonna have to meet Mr. Man soon," Dani said.

"Definitely," I told her. For the rest of our time together, Dani and I played catch-up with each other. When we parted ways, I was a little tipsy. The outside air felt amazing. I climbed into my car, rolled down the window, and sat there for a moment. I pulled out my phone and called Ace.

"What's up, mama?" he answered on the second ring.

"Hey," I slightly slurred.

"You good?"

"Yeah. I'm about to head home."

"Are you sure you can drive?" I heard him moving about in

his background. I chuckled and closed my eyes.

"I should be good. I'm not going far." I leaned back and closed my eyes, enjoying the breeze.

"Nah, stay right there, roll the windows up, and lock the doors. I'll be there in less than ten minutes."

"Nooo," I whined. "You don't have to drag Gabby outside. It's late." I hiccupped and giggled.

"She's with Deanna for tonight, so I'm literally just kicking it in the house. Don't move, Infinity. I'm not playing." Rather than respond, I chuckled. I was definitely feeling those drinks and it was probably best that I didn't drive.

"Okay, okay." I did as he said and cranked on the AC. I heard his car start and chuckled again because I couldn't believe he was coming all the way to the bar to drive my tipsy ass home. "How is my car going to get home?"

"My nigga lives around the corner, so he's gonna grab it and park it at his house. We'll pick it up tomorrow."

"Okay."

"Stay on the phone with me," he said. I smiled to myself but didn't say anything. I could hear the music playing lowly in the background, as well as the wind whipping from him driving with the window open. I closed my eyes and leaned my head back. Shortly after, I became startled by a soft tap on the window. As I looked, it was a man I remember seeing hanging with Ace before.

"I think your friend is here," I told him as I grabbed the stuff I needed to get out of the car.

"He is. I'm pulling up so come on." I spotted his headlights just as I reached for the door. I disconnected the call and climbed out. I smiled at his friend before I headed toward Ace's car. Before I could reach the door, he climbed out to open the door for me. I couldn't contain the smile that graced my face. "Get yo drunk ass in the car," he chuckled as he placed a kiss on my forehead.

"You missed me?"

"Always. Now let's go." Once I was in the car, I buckled up and closed my eyes as he pulled off. "You enjoy yourself?"

"I did. I haven't seen Dani in so long."

"Dani? Like a nigga?"

I tried to stifle my laugh, but I couldn't. I burst out laughing.

"No, like Danielle."

"I was about to say I know your ass ain't just play me like that."

"Awww, you were getting jealous," I joked as I leaned over the armrest to kiss his cheek.

"Nah, I'm not a jealous nigga. I'm confident in what I got, but I also don't have a problem checkin' a nigga about what's mine either."

"Oh, you're one of those that address the other dude?" I questioned, turning to face him.

"I approach all parties involved. I'll let the nigga know who I am, but then I would deal with you behind closed doors to let you go ahead and figure out what you wanted. I don't act a fool, but I make shit known," he explained. I nodded but didn't say anything. I continued to stare at him as he drove, and I was getting turned on. I bit the corner of my lip as I undressed him with my eyes. "Don't be eye-fuckin' me, Ma, unless you want me to pull this bitch over and knock that shit out the box."

I shrugged. "It ain't nothin'," I told him honestly.

"Shut your drunk ass up," he laughed. I rolled my eyes playfully and sat straight. The remainder of the ride to his house was quiet. I hadn't realized I dozed off until he tapped me. I looked around and noticed we were outside his place. "You couldn't even stay awake during the ride, and you wanted me to think you can handle this dick on the side of the road," he laughed.

"Shut up, I can handle it anywhere asshole," I playfully hit him as I climbed out of the car and made my way to his front door.

"Say whatever you want." He opened the door and went toward the kitchen as I headed to his bedroom to take a shower. I turned on the water and let it steam up the bathroom as I went and grabbed a pair of Ace's boxers with one of his t-shirts. I stripped in his bedroom and walked into the bathroom ass naked. Climbing under the water, I instantly relaxed. I closed my eyes and allowed the hot water to massage my body. It wasn't long before I felt a cool breeze and a chill swept over me, causing me to shiver.

"Any room for me?" he asked, closing the curtain behind him.

"Always." I turned around and faced him, running my hand down his buff chest. Although I had never seen him work out, there was no way he didn't with how in shape he was. I was tempted to lick his chest from top to bottom.

"What are you doing, girl?" he questioned.

"Shh," I told him as my hand trailed down his chest to his slightly bushy pubic hairs and his semi-hard dick. My mouth started watering at the feeling of the veins protruding from his member. I kept my eyes on his face and could see his breathing picking up. "What was all that shit you were spitting, sir?" I questioned as I began to slowly stroke him. Rather than say anything, he closed his eyes, leaned his head back, and took his bottom lip in between his teeth. I smirked and slowly descended to my knees. I took him into my mouth, and it was as if he became harder. As I slurped up and down his shaft, I took a peek at him and saw that he was using the wall to hold his balance. I gripped the back of his thighs as his hand found its way to the back of my head.

"Shit," I heard him just about whisper. His fingers became tangled in my hair as he guided my head back and forth. I allowed spit to dribble from my mouth and used it as a lubricant as I massaged his dick with my hand. I applied pressure at the base and turned it in the opposite direction of my mouth. I could feel his thighs tightening and knew he was holding back from busting. I moaned and then allowed his dick to touch the back of my throat before groaning on it. With some force, he pulled my head back and signaled for me to stand up. I wiped my mouth and before I could fully stand, he scooped me up. My legs wrapped around his waist, and he slipped himself right inside of me in one motion. I moaned and shifted a little to adjust to his size.

Not only did Ace have a good nine-inch dick, but he knew exactly what the fuck to do with it. I hugged him tightly, enjoying the ride I knew he was about to take my ass on.

"Oh, the dick got your tongue," he asked as he slowly rotated his hips. I gasped as I felt him hit my spot. "There she is," he growled, as he gripped my hips and turned around to place my back against the wall. Once he had me secure between his body and the wall, he wasted no time.

"Don't drop me," I managed to let out. The things he was doing to my body had me ready to tell him I would have every single baby he wanted to have.

"I would never. I'm just trying to see where all that mouth is now," he panted. Instead of responding, I grabbed his jaw and smashed my mouth into his. He didn't miss a beat as he continued hitting my spot. I felt the familiar feeling coming from my toes and shooting up my body. Behind my closed eye lids, I rolled my eyes and bit softly on his lip to keep from calling out. He slowed up and allowed me to catch my breath, but he never removed himself from me. "I hope you don't think we're done," he said turning around so my back was now facing the shower. He reached around me, shut the water off, and pulled the curtain back.

"What are you doing?"

"Seeing if you can back up all that shit you were talking. We can shower later." He stepped out of the shower, still holding me in the air. I tightened my grip on him and started bouncing slowly. "Chill out for a second," he said. I couldn't help but chuckle. He laid me softly on the bed. I could hear his central AC humming and the cool air mixed with my wet body caused my nipples to become rock hard. Once I was laid down, he kneeled on the bed and stared at me while slowly stroking.

By now, I had sobered up, but I was now on a dick high from that orgasm I had. Part of me wanted to tap out, but another part of me wanted him to fuck me rough and hard. He leaned over and placed one of my hard nipples in his mouth while he twirled the other one between two fingers and slow stroked. I couldn't stop my eyes from rolling and the way he was back tapping on my spot, I could hardly breathe.

"Breathe, mama," he spoke in my ear in a harsh whisper. That was it. I lost it. An orgasm ripped through me faster than I could think. "That's it. Good girl."

I needed him to shut up, immediately. He was bringing feelings over my body that I didn't know I could feel. My body shook for a few more seconds, but once I was able to feel my legs, I tapped him to signal him to move. When he leaned to the side, I pushed him down on his back and climbed on top. I slowly lowered myself on his erect dick and sucked in a breath as he stretched me back open. He instantly grabbed my hips. I planted my hands on my knees and began bouncing up and down. He closed his eyes and took his bottom lip in between his teeth. I smirked as I began tightening my muscles as I bounced up and down. I felt his grip on my hips tighten as he tried to slow me down, but I was in control here.

"Chill out," he hissed without opening his eyes. I didn't respond, but I felt his dick begin throbbing. I bounced harder and faster, clenching my walls tighter and that was it. Before he could form another word, he had shot off his load deep inside of me. I slowed down but kept slowly moving to ensure I was draining his ass. I collapsed on his chest, and he slowly ran his hands up and down my back as we enjoyed the high, we were coming down from. "You wild as shit, mama," he chuckled. I smiled and hugged him tighter but didn't say anything. We laid in silence for a few moments before I got up and headed back to the bathroom for a shower. It didn't take long before Ace joined me. We both quickly washed and got out. I noticed Ace changed the sheets. We bypassed putting on clothes and climbed into bed. Ace pulled me tightly into his body and it wasn't long before I was drifting off to sleep.

Chapter Twenty - Eight

Aaliyah Murphy

I sighed as I walked into my lawyer's office to meet with her regarding the custody case. I couldn't lie, I was nervous as hell. Although she was representing me, she knew just like I knew that me disappearing for a year was not a good look with me asking for custody. I took a deep breath as I sat in the chair and waited for them to call me.

"She'll take you now, Aaliyah," the paralegal notified me. I gave her a small smile before wiping my hands down my scrub pants and headed into her office.

"Hi, Aaliyah. How are you?" my lawyer, Carina Miller, greeted me.

"I'm okay. How are you?"

"Good, good. Here, have a seat. Let's talk." I took a seat and placed my keys in the available chair next to me. "Have you had any luck with seeing your daughter?" she questioned.

I sighed. "No. Her dad is pretty dead set on keeping me away."

"I see. I was able to pull up the court records for when he went, and he did everything the legal way, so to be honest, it's going to be a hard case."

I dropped my head and swallowed the lump that formed in my throat. This was what I feared.

"The paperwork shows that he has all say-so over the baby. He makes all decisions when it comes to her. To start, I don't think we should immediately go for custody."

"What? So I have to beg to see my child?" I damn near cried out.

"Beg, no. But seeing as how he has had her for more than a year and she is well taken care of, there is no reason for a judge to pull her from him. Unless you have some dirt on him that he has her in any sort of harm, or is a danger to her, they aren't going to take her from him. Our best bet would probably be to ask for visitation."

"What the fuck? I'm her mother! I'm not a guest. Visitation?"

Carina sighed. "Aaliyah, biologically, yes, you are her mother. On paper, you have no legal rights to her. I need you to remember that. Unfortunately, you must play by his rules. He calls the shots and trying to force things can make him shut down and keep you from her." I understood what she was saying, but I hated every damn minute of it. I wasn't a danger to my daughter, yet I had to be treated like one.

"How soon can we get this started?" I questioned. "I'm ready like yesterday to get involved with my daughter."

"The first mediation date is scheduled for two weeks from now. We'll pitch the idea of a few months of visitation and then see if we can ask for more."

"I gotta get visitation for months?" I screeched. This shit was worse than I thought.

"Aaliyah," she spoke before sighing.

"I know, I know. I don't really have a choice. How long do you think this will have to last?"

"I can't say. We have to prove to the judge that there is a benefit to you having joint custody of your daughter. The only thing I can say to begin is to keep trying but don't make things difficult. We'll get through this."

I gave a small smile, but I wasn't happy with the things she was saying. I knew I royally fucked myself, but I wasn't feeling this whole visitation and kissing ass thing. Carina and I spoke for a few more minutes before I left deeply in my feelings. I made it to my car, started the engine and cranked the AC. While waiting, I pulled out my phone and tried to text Ace although I figured he still had me blocked.

Me (1:12pm) – Hey, can we please talk? I know I owe both you and Gabrielle an apology, and I'm willing to do just that. I'm asking if you could please just give me a chance to prove I've changed, and I want to be involved in my daughter's life.

I hit send, and my eyes bucked when I saw my iMessage was

delivered. I was expecting for the message bubble to immediately turn green, but it didn't. I could hear my heart beating in my ears as I noticed the response bubbles start to jump.

Ace (1:13pm) – I'll let you know when I'm free.

I smiled brightly because I couldn't believe he actually answered me without cursing me out. Maybe could do this without court, but only time will tell.

*****

Three Days Later...

I was surprised to receive a text from Ace. Although it was last minute as shit, I forgot anything else I planned on doing, because he finally agreed to meet and talk to me. I only hoped he would be smart enough to bring my daughter with him because I desperately wanted to see her. Part of me thought about going to the daycare and trying to pick her up, but the last thing I needed was a kidnapping charge.

I pulled up to Roger Williams Park shortly after twelve and backed into a spot. I made sure to park in a spot where I could see the entrance when Ace pulled in. He told me he would meet me at 12:15. I couldn't lie, I was nervous as hell. It was clear that Ace and I didn't get along, but I hoped for the most part, today, we could start on clean feet and begin co-parenting.

I drummed my fingers against the steering wheel as I waited. I saw a black-on-black Jeep pull into the parking lot and sat up straight. It was hard to see in the windows due to the dark tint, but something told me it was Ace. I watched as he climbed out and walked around to the passenger side of the vehicle. Just as I was climbing out, I paused when I saw he wasn't alone. I spotted the girl I stopped in Walmart, and she was holding my daughter. I felt anger beginning to build up inside of me, but instead of reacting, I closed my eyes and counted to ten before I continued to climb out. I closed the door just as they were approaching my vehicle.

"Hi," I spoke.

"What's good?" Ace responded and his friend simply smiled. I was anxious and I wanted to hold my daughter. "Ma, can you take her to the playground for a little so I can talk to her?" he asked his friend. She simply responded sure before she and Gabrielle walked off. I couldn't lie, I was irritated. I didn't see the point in bringing his friend, or bringing my daughter if I couldn't bond with her. "What's up? You good?"

"Yeah," I sighed heavily. "Sorry. I was just a little taken aback that you weren't alone."

He chuckled. "I figured it would be cool to let Gabby run off some energy while we talked." I nodded and swallowed hard but didn't say anything else. "What did you wanna talk about?"

I shoved my hands in the back pockets of my jeans before I leaned against the hood of my car.

"I want to apologize. I know with a man like you that words mean nothing, but it's a start. I was wrong as hell. I thought the grass was greener on the other side, but it turned out it wasn't even close. Everything I thought I wanted, doesn't faze me anymore. However, I should have been woman enough to face you, and not leave her on the porch like that. I just didn't know how. I couldn't picture you looking at me with hatred in your eyes. I will say that I was selfish. I only thought about me. I never stopped to think about how my actions would affect not only you, but her as well. And for that, I deeply apologize.

"I truly mean it when I say that I've changed. I went to school where I obtained my medical assistant license, I have my own place and clearly my own car." I pointed towards the car. "It's not much, but it's all mine and I busted my ass to get it. All I'm asking for is just a chance to prove that I'm ready to be a mother and I will always, always put her first." I didn't realize I was crying until Ace reached over and wiped my face.

"I appreciate the apology, Liyah. I truly do. I'm also proud of you getting your life back on track, but I need you to understand why I have to move the way that I do. When we rocked with each other, we rocked with each other hard. Back then, I never saw myself without you. When you found out you were pregnant, I started seeing a selfish side of you that I never seen, and honestly, it fucked with me. The thought of you killin' my seed, literally took my breath away. When you disappeared, I was sick as fuck. I searched for you for weeks! I went days without sleeping trying to find you, to make sure you were good. It was literally as if you just vanished. All your people I thought fucked with me proved who their loyalty was to, and that's cool.

I expected nothing less because, as I said, those were your people. Every fuckin' day I prayed that you were good. I prayed that if my seed didn't make it, that you were at least good.

"To wake up and find a baby on my damn doorstep with a note and some diapers, fucked me up. I felt a mix of emotions I couldn't even explain. It literally was the weirdest shit I've ever fuckin' dealt with, but I thank you. While I won't ever agree with how you handled shit, I thank you for not harming her, and actually keeping her. That little girl is the best fuckin' thing that's ever happened to me. Parenting is the hardest shit I've ever fuckin' done, but it's rewarding as hell. There were many days where I wished you could experience all of the firsts that I did, but then at the same time, I began to question how you could do the shit you did. I couldn't understand and part of me still doesn't. Hell, I probably never will, but it's not for me to understand. It's something you have to live with. Over the last few months, I've tossed back and forth if I even wanted to get to this point, but then I realized it's not about me. It's about Gabby, and I know one day she will have questions and unfortunately, I won't be the one that has answers. I also don't want her to feel like I kept her from you.

"I only ask one thing, Aaliyah. Do not hurt my baby girl. I don't give a shit what happens because if you do," he stepped closer to me, closing the gap between us and whispering into my ear. "I will slaughter you and your family will never fuckin' find you." When he stepped back and I looked into his eyes, I shuddered at the look I saw. If I ever thought about playing with him before, his look spoke volumes.

"I would never," I said just above a whisper. I meant what I was saying. I desperately wanted to be involved in my baby's life. I wouldn't do anything to risk it. "Thank you, Ace. You don't know how much this means to me," I sniffled. He didn't say anything else, but I noticed he looked toward the playground where his friend and my daughter was. He started walking in that direction, so I followed behind him. I would be lying if I said I wasn't nervous as hell. I wiped my hands down my pants as the friend met us, holding hands with my daughter. I smiled as Ace picked her up and planted a kiss on her cheek.

"Gabby, this is your mom," he introduced us. I couldn't stop the tears that welled in my eyes. I don't know why I was expecting him to introduce me as Aaliyah, but it warmed my heart that he introduced me as her mom.

"Mmmm," she stared at Ace.

"Mama," he said to her.

"Mama," she repeated.

"Hi, pretty." I reached out to touch her face and she dropped her head on her dad's shoulder. I felt a kind of way, but I knew it would take time. "Can I hold you?" I asked her. She lifted her head and looked at Ace as if she were wanting permission. He gave her a small nod before leaning towards me. To my surprise, she came to me with no problem. I noticed his friend smile before she leaned and whispered in his ear. He handed her his keys, and she walked off, which I appreciated.

I closed my eyes and hugged my daughter tightly. The tears that were sitting in my eyes, rapidly fell down my cheeks. I went over to the table and bench that was within the playground and sat down. I sat her on my lap and stared in her face. I couldn't stop crying, even if I tried too.

"Play?" she spoke.

"You want to go play?" She nodded her head. "Can I join you?" She nodded her head again. I put her down on the ground and allowed her to run around as she held my hand. I had longed for moments like this, and I could only hope that this would be the first of many more playdates to come.

Chapter Twenty - Nine

Deandre 'Ace' Lemetti

I sat on the bench and watched Aaliyah and Gabby run around the playground. This was the shit I longed for, from the moment Aaliyah told me she was pregnant. I pulled out my phone and saw a text from Infinity.

Wifey (2:18pm) – *I'm glad you decided to go through with this. I know the decision wasn't easy, but they look to be truly enjoying themselves.*

I smirked as I began to respond.

Me (2:19pm) – *Yeah, I just hope it remains this way. I would hate for her to get used to her, then she up and leaves. Also, thank you for coming with me. I appreciate that shit more than you know.*

I hit send and locked my phone as I went back to watching Gabby and her mom laugh together. Initially, Infinity didn't want to come with me, but I wanted her mainly to keep Gabby busy while I spoke to Aaliyah. I didn't know how the conversation would go and didn't want to experience us arguing. I was surprised when she walked away to allow Aaliyah and Gabby privacy to bond.

Wifey (2:21pm) – *Of course. I told you that I'll always be your support system and let's remain positive. It looks to be starting well, so let's keep the thoughts that it will remain this way. I'm gonna take a nap. Let me know when it's time to go.*

I responded telling her that I would and locked my phone. I sat on the bench for another almost two hours until Aaliyah brought Gabby over to me as Gabby rubbed her face.

"I think she's tired," she spoke as Gabby rested her head on Aaliyah's shoulder.

"Probably. She's usually had a nap by now." I stood up and she handed Gabby to me.

"Thank you, again. I really appreciate you giving me a shot to prove to you that I've changed."

"It's really not me that you have to prove it to at this point. You gotta prove it to her. Like I said, I just ask that you remain consistent with her."

"I promise I will. I usually work during the week until no later than five and I'm free on the weekends," she explained.

"A'ight, bet. I'll be in touch."

"O-okay." She leaned in and kissed Gabby's cheek, telling her she loved her before I watched her walk off towards her car. Once I saw she was in her car and straight, Gabby and I headed to my truck. Infinity was passed out with the front seat reclined, and I couldn't do anything but chuckle. I unlocked the door, and placed Gabby in her seat. Once I strapped her in, I circled the car and climbed in, tapping Infinity's leg to let her know we were back in the car.

"Dang, how long have I been sleep?" she asked stretching and wiping her face.

"A good two hours."

"Damn, we've been here that long?" I nodded. She looked over her shoulder and saw that Gabby was in her seat. "How did it go?"

"Better than I expected. Gabby seemed to enjoy herself and that's what matters."

"How are you going to set a schedule with her?" she asked.

"I don't know yet. I want a few more of these and then maybe we'll do some day visits for a few hours." Part of me truly wanted to be selfish, but I knew in the long run that if Aaliyah truly did change, it would be beneficial to Gabby.

"Just take it one day at a time, babe. You don't have to figure it all out today." I offered her a smile as we made our way back to my spot.

*****

Two Weeks Later...

"You have everything you need?" I asked Infinity as I grabbed the handle of her suitcase.

"I think so. If I don't, then I don't need it," she shrugged. She hit the light switch and we headed towards the door.

Today was the day we were leaving for Infinity's birthday trip. I hadn't told her where we were going. Instead, I just told her to make sure she had her passport, and that she should pack enough outfits for a five-day trip, plus at least one formal outfit, and some bathing suits. We were heading to Miami to board a five-night cruise that was stopping in two islands of the Bahamas and Grand Turk, Turks & Caicos. I had never been, but I had scoped it out for a little bit. I booked an excursion to fuck with some dolphins, but honestly., I didn't know if I was gonna be able to get down with that shit.

"Are you going to tell me where we're going?" she asked.

"Nah, mama. You'll find out when we get to the airport." I didn't miss her rolling her eyes, but I chuckled. My mama, thankfully, was able to take the week from work to keep Gabby for me. I knew during the day she was going to ship her ass off to daycare still. Gabby was on the move and kept a nigga on his toes. Honestly, though, I wouldn't have had it any other way.

Within twenty minutes, we were pulling into the airport parking garage. I luckily found a spot not too far from the terminal entrance. Infinity stood off to the side to talk to her mother and I checked in the bags, which worked out because the gentleman mentioned our destination. Just as she was done, the gentleman dropped the bags on the conveyor belt, and I grabbed Infinity's hand. I was surprised that the TSA line wasn't full. I knew with the TSA check I would have to reveal where we were heading. I handed Infinity her boarding pass. She damn near snatched it from my hand to see the destination.

"Fort Lauderdale?" she questioned.

"Yup."

I didn't miss the slight disappointment that graced her face. I tried to stifle my laugh as we made it to the TSA agent and handed her our licenses.

"Cheer up," I told her as we placed our stuff in the bin. She gave me a small smirk. I shook my head and chuckled as I walked through the metal detector. Once Infinity came through, we grabbed our carry-on bags and headed toward the gate. "You really sitting here all pissy in the face?" I asked her.

She sighed. "I'm grateful. I was expecting out of the country, however, I can't complain because you didn't have to do anything, so thank you."

"Since you've met me, have I disappointed you?" I looked at her sideways. She shook her head. "Exactly. Trust your nigga, mama. I promise, I got you. I'm about to make your twenty-fifth birthday memorable."

"Okay."

We stopped at the Dunkin' spot and she grabbed a coffee and sandwich, and I just grabbed a bottle of water. Our flight was scheduled to board within an hour, and we had a straight flight. If all went well, we would make it to the terminal around one.

Four hours later, we landed at Fort Lauderdale International

Airport. So far, we were on time for everything. My mama tried to tell me to fly in the day before, but I pushed it by flying in the same day. I wasn't going to lie; I was praying like hell that everything continued smoothly, and we would make the ship. Thankfully, they had a ride-share area right outside the airport so as soon as I requested one, the ride was immediately accepted, and the driver was there. Rushing in the hot ass sun, we easily spotted the driver. Once he got out and helped me load the luggage, we were off.

"Are you ready to tell me the plans?" Infinity asked.

"Nope. Just sit back and chill."

I didn't miss her rolling her eyes as she sighed, placed her AirPods in her ear and looked out the window. I wasn't gonna front. It was killing me to not tell her, but I truthfully wanted her to be surprised.

I was shooting my mother a text when I saw Infinity shoot up in her seat. Looking up, I saw that we were pulling up to the Port of Miami.

"W-what is this?" she stuttered. "We're going on a cruise?" she questioned, looking at me. I just smiled at her. "Shut up! We're really going on a cruise?"

"Yeah," I chuckled.

"Oh my fucking God!" She began doing a little dance in her seat, and truth be told, her excitement did something to a nigga. "What islands are we stopping at? How long are we going to be gone? How the fuck did you pull this off?"

"What do you want me to answer first?" I responded as the driver pulled over. There were a few gentlemen at the curb that looked to be ready to push the luggage toward the boat. Rather than check ours, we decided to keep ours. Rooms were typically ready by one, so by the time we cleared security and made it on the boat, we could head straight to our room.

"I can't believe this," she said in awe as she looked around. "How did you pull this off?"

"I got ways. Your nigga knows how to get shit done."

"Who helped you?" she quizzed.

"Damn, why somebody had to help me? I couldn't have just done this on my own?"

"Usually Deanna helps you plan shit. That's why I'm asking."

"For your information, it was my idea and besides island suggestions, I did everything myself. Thanks for the credit," I stated sarcastically.

"Aww, don't be like that. I appreciate this babe, for real." She grabbed my arm to stop me from walking and planted a kiss on my lips. We continued to the boat and within twenty-five minutes, we were boarding as I pulled the suitcases behind me. Infinity immediately started taking pictures and videos as we made our way. After doing the little security check shit on the boat, we headed towards our room. The boat hadn't even taken off yet, but I could tell the money I dropped on this trip would be well worth it. Infinity's reaction to everything told me so. I couldn't wait to explore these islands with my lady and have some nasty ass sex all through the room we had.

Chapter Thirty

Infinity Morrison

One Week Later…

The vibration of my phone woke me up from the deepest sleep I had gotten within the last week. We returned home from our trip yesterday and I was beat. The cruise was everything I could have ever imagined and then some. I had never seen crystal blue water until I stepped foot on those Caribbean beaches. Everything from the balcony cabin Ace booked to the dolphin encounter excursion on Nassau Island was amazing. I truly had never been on a better trip. Add the sex we had, especially on the balcony in the middle of the night, the shit was beyond amazing. I was already lowkey plotting to find another cruise to go on.

Now that we've returned, I was trying to catch up on sleep, but whoever was on the other end of my phone was not respecting that. I let it roll over to voicemail hoping that the caller would get the hint, but they didn't. Instead, they called right back. Without opening my eyes, I reached over to the nightstand next to my bed and felt around for my phone. Once it was in my hand, I slid my finger across the screen and placed the phone to my ear without saying anything.

"Hello," I heard my mother's voice boom through the phone.

"Hi, ma."

"Are you still in bed?"

"Yes."

"Why?"

"Because I'm tired. What's up?" I questioned as I yawned. If it were anyone else asking me these questions, I would have hung up the phone. However, I was trying to give my mother the benefit of the doubt.

"I was calling to see if you wanted to do lunch so you can tell me about your trip, but maybe we can do dinner," she suggested.

"Dinner sounds great. I'll call you when I wake up. Love you."

"Love you too."

I locked my phone and slid it under my pillow as I tried to fall back to sleep. It was short-lived when I felt my blanket being pulled off me. I knew it was nobody but Ace since he was the only one who had a key to my townhouse.

"Rise and shine, beautiful," he spoke.

"It's too early," I groaned, yanking the blanket back and

tossing it over my head.

"Too early? Mama, it's almost one in the afternoon."

"What?" I jumped up. "How the heck did I sleep so late?"

"Because between the enjoyment of the trip and being jetlagged, you haven't rested the way you need too." He sat on the edge of the bed as I stood and stretched. I headed into the bathroom to relieve my bladder and handle my hygiene. "You wanna grab a bite to eat?" he questioned.

"I'll find something in the kitchen. My mom wants to go out to dinner later, so I'm not gonna fill up now," I let him know.

"Bet. I can order a pizza or something."

"That's fine. Just order me some wings. Where's Gabby?"

"In the living room in her chair. We just came from a playdate with her mom this morning."

"How did that go?"

"It wasn't bad. They seem to be building a nice little bond, which is cool."

"Are y'all still going through courts?"

"Yeah, our court date is actually tomorrow. I want shit in writing so she can't try and switch up or pull no fuck shit or nothing like that. It's all to protect my daughter," he explained. I nodded as I understood where he was coming from. His daughter's mother randomly appears and wants to be a mom; it's hard not to believe she has ulterior motives.

"Oh okay." Once I came out of the bathroom, I went over and sat on Ace's lap and planted kisses on his lips. "Thank you again for the trip. I enjoyed myself beyond words. I appreciate you, babe."

"Of course. You only turn twenty-five once, so it was only right I did something special. I'm glad you enjoyed yourself." We shared a few more kisses before we retreated into the living room with Gabby who was eating a few of her snacks that Ace had given her. We both climbed on the couch and waited for the food to come. By the time it arrived, Gabby was ready for a nap, and although I had just woken up, I wanted to join her. Instead, Ace and I enjoyed the quiet time as we ate, watched movies, and caught a quickie or two.

*****

A Few Hours Later...

I walked into Hook & Reel and looked around for my mother. It didn't take me long to find her since the restaurant wasn't full. I pointed to her, letting the hostess know that I was all set. As I approached her table, she stood to greet me.

"You're glowing, Fin! Not sure if it's the Caribbean suntan you got or what," my mother said. I smiled and brushed her off. I had definitely caught a tan because that sun on the boat and the islands was no joke. "How was the trip?" she asked as we sat down.

"Mom, it was amazing! I'm honestly upset that I didn't do it sooner." As soon as I finished my statement, the waitress came by and took my order. "You gotta go on one for real!"

"I'll definitely look into it. I always see the commercials and they look fun, but I've just never booked one."

"You definitely need to," I reiterated. The waitress returned with my drink while my mother and I sat catching up. I filled her in on how well the center was doing, and my relationship with Ace. She had met him a few times and from those few occasions, she actually liked him, which was big for me because my mom's opinion meant a lot. For the next two hours, my mother and I enjoyed each other's company as well as stuffing our faces with seafood boils and mixed drinks. There was nothing like spending time with my mom and I made a mental note to do it more often. Although we both had fairly busy schedules, I needed to find a way to make more time for her because she deserved it.

Once we parted ways, I drove home in silence. I couldn't stop the smile that graced my face as I thought back to the trip I had just returned from. One thing was for sure, I wouldn't wait so long to take another trip. If anyone deserved to see the world, it was me. Whether I was with somebody or traveling solo, I planned on stamping up my passport as soon as possible.

Chapter Thirty - One
Aaliyah Murphy

I wiped the lone tear that slipped from my eye as I walked out of the courtroom. Although my lawyer warned me about how this would go, it didn't hurt any less. Ace had been allowing Gabby and I to have playdates several times a week, but I had yet to have my daughter alone. Based on what the judge just said, it would be a while before that were to happen.

Apparently, Ace had me served shortly after I had left Gabby in his care. But because the only address he had was my mother's, I never received it. Since I didn't respond, he was granted full and sole custody, meaning he called all the shots. If he decided he no longer wanted me to see Gabby, I couldn't. I almost felt as if I had to kiss his ass and I wasn't a fan of that.

Like I said, thankfully, so far it had been smooth. However, I hated the fact that he had the ability to change his mind if he wanted to. According to the judge, our court order was supervised visitations once a week for three hours in a public setting of Ace's choice. We would then return in two months for an update and see if we could move to unsupervised visits, and then eventually overnights. It was all fuckin' stupid to me. These assholes acted as if I was a danger to my child.

I scoffed as I pushed the door open to the garage area of the courthouse. I didn't even stay back to speak to my lawyer. This was a bunch of bullshit, and I was regretting even hiring the bitch and going through with this. I had a better deal outside of court than I did at court. I shook my head, and just as I hit the unlock button on my key fob, I heard my name being called. Turning around, I spotted Ace jogging up to me.

"Damn, you left quick as hell," he said, breathing slightly heavy.

"Yeah, I'm sure you know I hate the agreement they put in place," I told him.

"I know, but I wanted to let you know I'm not going to change what we have going on now. We can keep the several days a week, schedule permitting. I would hate to go from three to four days a week, down to one. It's not fair to you or Gabby. I'm all about consistency with her, and that's too big of a change in my opinion." I nodded but didn't say anything. Although our co-parenting relationship was rocky, I was thankful for him because Ace could have continued to be an asshole. Instead, he decided to take the high road and I appreciated him for it.

"Thank you for that. I'm sorry for even getting this shit

started," I sighed. "I was just desperate and felt like I had nowhere else to turn," I told him honestly.

"I get it and I'll admit I may have been thinking irrationally. My only concern has always been Gabby. Was I pissed when you left her? Absolutely, and not because you didn't want to raise her, but because of how you left her. I let that dictate how I reacted, and I can admit that it may not have been the best. Eventually, it'll all work out. Get home safe." I nodded and watched as he walked off. I can admit, I breathed a little easier knowing that Ace was going to keep our current schedule in place because I would hate to see my baby girl less and less because a judge said so. While I may not have liked the outcome of court, I was definitely going to abide by it. I fucked up once, I wasn't about to do that shit again.

Chapter Thirty - Two

Deandre 'Ace' Lemetti

Three Months Later...

I used my key to let myself into Infinity's townhouse while carrying a sleeping Gabby. She had just come from spending the day with her mother. We recently went back to court and since we had no negative reports, the judge allowed unsupervised visits. I had to admit, the Aaliyah who left my daughter on my doorstep, was not the same Aaliyah now. She had truly done a complete one-eighty, and I was glad. While my daughter had positive female role models in her life, there was nothing like a mother's love. Gabby was adjusting to her nicely, and they both seemed to enjoy their time together.

I used my foot to close the door behind me. It was only then that I spotted Infinity sleeping on the couch. I looked at the cable box and saw it was only shortly after eight at night. I had just spoken to Infinity and told her that I was on the way, so I damn sure wasn't expecting her to be sleeping. Rather than wake her up, I headed to the spare bedroom that she had me put up a crib for Gabby in, and quickly placed Gabby in her crib. Thankfully Aaliyah had bathed Gabby so she would be out for the night.

Making my way back into the living room, I gently tapped Infinity until she woke.

"Hey, when did you get here?" she questioned as she looked around and then stretched.

"We just got here. You fell asleep quick as hell, huh?"

"Yeah, I guess." She wiped the drool from the corner of her mouth before she stood. "I hadn't even realized I had fallen asleep. I've been ridiculously tired lately."

"It's unusual because you've been sleeping like crazy too." I sat on the couch next to her and pulled her into my lap.

"I know."

The room went silent between us before she spoke.

"Did you eat?"

"Nah. Aaliyah said she fed Gabby, so I figured either you cooked, or we would order something."

"Let me go see what I have quick."

As she walked away, I eyed her body and could see the physical changes. Infinity was pregnant. I didn't know if she knew it or not, but the way her hips spread, her ass could hardly stay awake, and as I thought about it, it had been a long while since she mentioned having her period.

"Aye, mama," I called out before standing to my feet and following her. "Let me ask you something."

"Go ahead."

"When's the last time you had your period?"

"Last month," she answered quickly.

"You sure about that?" She paused what she was doing and kept her back to me. I smirked because I knew at that moment she truly was thinking about when the last time was. She stopped what she was doing and pulled out her phone. I rested against the dining room chair as I looked at her.

"Oh my God," she paused. Her hands shot to her mouth before she took off running towards her bedroom. I was stuck for a moment because I didn't know if I should have followed her or given her a second. After standing there for another few seconds, I headed in her direction. I found her in the bathroom sitting on the toilet with an empty pregnancy test box on the counter.

"Where the hell did you get that?" I laughed.

"Shut up. I always keep one on hand because you just never know." She finished going to the bathroom, but instead of wiping herself and getting up, she sat there staring at the test.

"What does it say?"

Instead of responding, she gasped. She continued to stare at the test, and I noticed a tear run down her cheek. I pushed myself off the doorframe and made my way into the bathroom. She wasn't speaking, so I reached out and grabbed the test from her hands. Clear as day, two pink lines stared back at me. My lip curled into a crooked smile, but I didn't want to get too excited until I knew for sure how she felt. I placed the test on the box sitting on the sink, and squatted down in front of her, taking her hands into mine.

"Look at me," I stated. With a tear-stained face, her eyes met mine. "What's going through your mind?"

"Everything! I'm happy, I'm scared, I want to scream, but I don't know if it's out of fear or excitement. I'm feeling like a million different emotions at once," she explained.

I understood what she was saying. She had only been pregnant once before and it ended in a tragedy for her. Her apprehension was normal, but I was here to rock by her side through it all.

"Remove every negative thought from your head. This baby will make it to term, and this baby will be everything you have dreamed of. There isn't a thing in this pregnancy you'll have to do alone, besides wipe your shitty ass after using the toilet." She laughed as she wiped her eyes. "Listen to me, mama. I know how bad you want this. From what you've told me, you've prayed for this. You've helped me with my daughter more than I can imagine. I see how you are with the kids at your center. You're made for this, mama. You're made to be an amazing mother, and I'm glad that we get to experience this together."

I leaned in and kissed the tears from her cheeks. She slowly nodded in understanding before I stood up and allowed her to finish in the bathroom. I took another look at the test and silently prayed to God that everything would be okay. It would be a lot to watch Infinity go through a tragedy. Even after all these years, her son was still a sensitive topic, so I don't think she could handle going through that again.

She stood up, wiped herself and washed her hands. I could read her face and see that she was lost in thought, but she also looked like she had something heavy on her mind.

"Aye," I called out to get her attention. "Talk to me." It was crazy how I could read her so easily. She would try hard to keep her thoughts and emotions to herself, but she wore them on her face, and I don't even think she realized it.

She sighed. "I just want to keep everything under wraps. I know you're close to your mom and Deanna, and I know you would want to tell them, but I would hate to go and tell everyone, and something happens."

"Don't worry about all that. Knowing what you've gone through, telling everyone isn't a priority. You and our baby's health are key. They can wait," I assured her. She gave me a small smile as we walked out of the bathroom. I peeked in the spare bedroom and checked on Gabby who was still asleep. I then went into Infinity's room where she was climbing into bed.

"So forget about cooking, huh?" I chuckled.

"Shit, sorry." She started to climb out of bed.

"Don't worry about it. I'll order something. Do you want anything?"

"What are you gonna order?"

"I don't know yet. Do you have a taste for anything?" She shook her head no. She laid down in bed and I sat on the opposite side while scrolling through the DoorDash app. Nothing seemed to appeal to me, so I closed it out before I got up and headed to the kitchen. I went through the cabinets and found a few boxes of cereal. Before pouring a bowl, I double checked to see if she had milk, which she did. I quickly grabbed the box of Cap'n Crunch Berries, the milk and a bowl and made myself some. I figured Infinity was back to sleep, so I sat in the kitchen and ate. I let my mind run over the fact that she was pregnant. I was excited. Gabby was still young, so I knew raising two kids under two wouldn't be the easiest. However, I knew for a fact Infinity was the one I wanted to go through this with. She was literally perfect for me…for us.

I finished my bowl of cereal and washed the bowl out. I pulled out my phone and shot Los a text. I knew I needed to get out of the streets, but I was dragging my feet with doing so. With Infinity being pregnant, the last thing I needed was her being stressed about me and wondering if I was okay. I was letting Los know that I was walking away and leaving it all to him. I had my run, and it was an excellent run, but I needed to get out before my time was up.

Once I was done texting, I headed into Infinity's room and just like I knew, she had passed out. I smirked before grabbing underclothes and heading to the bathroom to shower. I didn't know what God had in store for me, but I was ready for whatever road he was about to lead me down.

*****

The Next Day...

Infinity and Gabby were off to the center bright and early. I had gotten Gabby ready while Infinity yawned and got herself ready. Once I got Gabby strapped into her seat, I sent her and Infinity off with a shit ton of kisses. I went back into the house, got dressed, and headed to my own crib. I had been kickin' it at Infinity's crib for a few days, so I had to at least, check my mail.

I stopped at Dunkin' and grabbed a coffee before reaching my spot. I could see my mailbox overflowing and figured the majority was nothing but bills. Killing the engine, I climbed out, activated the alarm, and headed toward the door. Nosey-ass Mrs. Graham was outside rocking in her rocking chair, so I waved to her.

"Good morning! How's that sweet baby girl of yours?" she asked.

"She's doing good, Mrs. Graham. She's getting big."

"Enjoy it, son, it goes by so fast."

"I will. You have a good day," I stated, ending the conversation. I grabbed my mail and headed inside, locking the door behind me. As I flipped through, I dropped the bills on the table, making a mental note to ensure all were paid. An envelope with my name and address written by hand in blue ink caught my attention. The return address didn't have a name, just an address.

I was skeptical about opening it. While I typically stayed to myself, niggas couldn't be trusted and I'm sure a nigga had some sort of enemies.

I eyed the envelope for a few more seconds before I opened it. I pulled out the single sheet and my eyes scanned the letter. I twisted my face slightly and then my eyed damn near bugged out of my head. This shit had to be a joke. I quickly removed my phone from my pocket. Just as I was about unlock my phone to dial up my mother, Deanna's name flashed across my screen.

"What's up, sis?" I answered.

"Uhh, question. Did you get a letter in the mail today from a lawyer's office?"

"I did, and I was about to call Ma about it. Why?"

"Because I got one too. Did you read the letter?"

"I did."

"Alright, hold on." The line went silent, but I saw the call was still connected so I figured she was calling my mother.

"Ma," she returned to the line.

"What child?"

"Are you home?"

"I'm pulling up now. Why?"

"Alright, grab your mail and tell me what's in it?"

As they went back and forth, I grabbed my cup of coffee and sat at the counter, placing the phone on speaker as I silently reread the letter.

"Why do you want to know what mail is at my house,

Deanna?"

"Can you please just stop asking questions and do it."

I heard my mother sigh and I chuckled. I knew she wanted to curse Deanna out, but she was too nosey to not figure out what Deanna was looking for. I could hear her keys jingling, so I knew she was out of the car. I remained silent as I heard her close the mailbox and then let herself into her house. The clanking of the keys on the table let us know that she was now going through her mail. I held my breath as I waited for her response.

"My light bill, my gas bill, my phone bill, and..." She went silent.

"And what?" I asked.

"Deandre?"

"Hey, mama. What else do you got there?"

"Something from the Law Offices of Smith, Jones and Brown."

"Open yours and read it please," Deanna stated.

"What is this?"

"That's what we're trying to figure out."

The line remained silent as I assumed my mother read the letter. I heard her gasp.

"Does yours say you have an inheritance of one point five million dollars?" my sister questioned.

"Mine says one million, but who the fuck? What the hell is this?"

"Sounds like one of us needs to make a call because this is crazy."

"I'll call you back," my mother relayed to us before ending the call. Deanna and I remained on the phone in silence.

"Dre, this is life-changing," she said.

"I'm just confused. Dad's been gone for well over twenty years and now all of a sudden on the same day, all of us get a letter in the mail that we have inheritances totaling four million dollars combined?"

"I am too. I'm gonna call them myself because I gotta figure out what this is about," Deanna told me. "I'll call you as soon as I get some answers."

"Bet." We ended the call, and I sat there staring at the letter. The only thing I could think of was my dad had some sort of business he left behind, but it wouldn't make sense as to how she wouldn't have known about it. I wasn't about to stress myself out about it though. I ran upstairs to grab more clothes to bring to Infinity's spot so I could exchange what I had there. I had to chuckle to myself because I had this whole ass crib, but we spent the majority of our time at her townhouse. I couldn't even front though; I loved the home feel her spot had.

Twenty-five minutes later, I was heading out the door to meet up with Los. It was time for me to let him know my plans because I had to make some legitimate moves. With another baby on the way, there was no way that I was remaining in this street shit. I risked my life enough, but I was done. I knew Los would handle the shit with no problem though. I pulled out my burner and shot him a text letting him know that I was on the way.

As soon as I pulled out of the driveway, my phone rang. Looking at the dashboard, I saw it was Deanna.

"Hello."

"I finally got through. They want us to meet at their office at three this afternoon." Looking at the time, I had a few hours to spare.

"Did they tell you what it was about?"

"Nope, they wouldn't say. I already texted mama. She's not answering my calls. I'm gonna give her another thirty minutes and if I call her again and she doesn't answer, I'm popping up." I couldn't help but laugh because I knew Deanna was serious. She didn't play about my mama not answering her phone, especially when she wasn't at work."

"A'ight, I'll meet you there. Shoot me the address."

"Will do."

We ended the call just as I turned onto Los' block. I looked around and realized how dead it was, which was weird. An eerie feeling came over me just as I pulled to a stop in front of Los' spot. I looked around again. I couldn't shake the feeling. I was about to put the car into park, but something told me keep it pushing. I pulled out my phone and realized Los hadn't responded. Glancing up at his crib, his car wasn't in the driveway either. Dialing his number, I pulled away from his spot.

"Yo," he answered.

"Where you at?"

"The spot."

"Damn. I'm just leaving your crib. Did the boys fall through here recently or something?" I questioned as I headed toward his stash spot.

"Not that I know of." Before I could respond, I heard nothing but sirens. Looking around, I thought they may have been coming for me, but I noticed them screeching halt in front of Los' spot.

"Yo, they pulling up to your crib," I notified him as I pulled over.

"What the fuck?" I didn't respond. Instead, I tapped the FaceTime icon so he could see. When he answered, I flipped the camera so he could see it. They swarmed out of their vehicles and toward his house like a group of marching ants. "What the fuck is happening?" Los roared. I killed the engine and climbed out of the vehicle as I walked back down the street. I could hear Los putting shit away and I knew he was trying to rush here. It wasn't long before they battery rammed his door down and went inside with guns drawn. "Nigga, go talk to them or some shit. Why the fuck are you just standing there?" he hollered.

"Fuck you want them to shoot me? Hell naw."

I saw an officer standing by his vehicle watching.

"Ayo," I called out. "Can you tell me what's going on?"

"Execution of a search warrant?"

"For what though? What are they looking for?"

"Why? Are you the owner?" he asked, looking in my direction.

"Nah, but it's rare you see someone's damn door being bulldozed down in the middle of the day."

"He ain't the owner, but I am," Los hollered.

"Excuse me?" the officer questioned.

"My homeboy owns the house y'all just entered and he ain't even there."

The officer looked at me before calling over his walkie-talkie that the homeowner wasn't there.

"Now can you tell me what the fuck is up?" Los questioned. I turned the camera to face the officer.

"Sir, where are you?"

"Nah the real fuckin' question is what the fuck are y'all looking for that y'all pig ass bitches are trashing my fuckin' house."

"If you can meet us at the station, we can answer any questions that you may have." I looked the officer up and down before my eyes landed on his badge that had the last name Harris on it.

"Fuck the station! I'm coming right the fuck there and y'all better have a legitimate ass reason to do what the fuck y'all doing or else I'm hitting the department with a hefty fuckin' repair bill." The call ended before Officer Harris could say anything else. I shook my head and shoved my hands in my pockets as I stood there and waited for Los. I knew he was about to pull up on a thousand, so I hung around to try and keep him as calm as possible. Just as Los came flying around the corner, damn near on two wheels, my phone rang again. Pulling it out of my pocket, I saw it was Mrs. Graham.

"Hey, Mrs. Graham. What's up?"

"There is a swarm of officers that just showed up at your house," she announced. Immediately, my blood ran warm, and I was now seeing red. For both mine and Los' houses to be hit on the same day meant that there was somebody out here on some fuck shit. One thing was for sure, I was gonna find out who the fuck was behind it.

Chapter Thirty - Three

Deanna Lemetti

It was two fifty and I was sitting in the parking lot of this lawyer's office. I had been trying to call my brother, but he wasn't answering. My mother had already told me that she was on her way. I dialed Deandre's number again but was met with the voicemail. He knew this was important so I didn't know what could have had him tied up. I sighed heavily. I spotted my mother pulling into the parking lot, so I killed the engine to get out and meet her. Walking over to her car, I stood at the trunk as she gathered her stuff to climb out.

"Hey," she greeted, giving me a cheek-to-cheek kiss. "Where's your brother?"

"I have no idea. I've been trying to call him, but his phone is going to voicemail." My mother shook her head.

"Ain't no telling with that man. Let's go inside. If he doesn't show, then we'll just fill him in." I nodded and followed my mother's lead inside. Walking to the receptionist's desk, my mother let her know who we were and the receptionist told us to have a seat while she got Mr. Jones for us. I would be lying if I said I wasn't nervous. I won't front, my mother and I did well for ourselves. Between our jobs and Deandre making sure we were good, we wanted for nothing. Neither of us approved of Deandre's lifestyle, but we also couldn't force him to do anything different. I just hoped that for Gabby's sake, he would walk away from this shit soon.

Just as we sat down, an older gentleman came out of his office towards where we were sitting.

"Mrs. Lemetti?" he inquired, and my mom nodded. "Follow me."

My mother and I stood and followed the gentleman to his office. He pointed to the seats in front of the desk as he made his way around.

"I'm sure you're wondering what is going on, so I won't waste any time. My name is Daniel Jones, and I'm a partner here at Smith, Jones, and Brown. I was also a business partner of your husband over thirty years ago," he revealed. My eyes bucked and I looked over at my mom.

"Excuse me, what? My husband didn't own a business," my mother clarified.

Mr. Jones cleared his throat, loosened his tie, and then looked between the two of us.

"Before I became a lawyer, I was into the streets as a young buck. Darius Lemetti and I met in high school. It wasn't until we graduated and had no idea what we wanted to do, that we became runners for the local dealers. We quickly worked our way up, and within eighteen months, we were running shit. We had money pouring in so damn fast, we had no idea how to properly handle it. I began doing research and decided to invest in some real estate. I've been a landlord and flipping houses for decades. About four years in, Darius met you and he told me he was walking. He took what he had and kept it moving. I wasn't mad at him and respected his decision. He found the one for him and wanted to settle down.

"I vowed to myself that I wouldn't have any of that shit without Darius, so I stacked some shit on the side for him. My goal was to let it get to a few million dollars and break him off with that shit. He deserved it. When he was killed, it was a huge blow. I didn't come up to you all, but I did attend his services After he died, I vowed to get out of the streets. Darius always told me I was better than the streets. The problem was, I wasn't searching for anything beyond the streets. After he died, I did a lot of soul-searching. I had to dig deep within myself and find what I enjoyed doing. It didn't take me long to realize law was my passion. As you can see, I've come pretty far."

"I see that," my mother voiced. "I'm still confused at how you pop up all of these years later and hand out funds."

He nodded in understanding. "Right. When I started seeing huge profits from my real estate business, I needed ways to continue to make money. That's the hustler in me, I need multiple streams of income. I started investing in stocks. At the time, I didn't know shit about it except it could be hit or miss. I found a trustworthy broker, and let's just say over the years, he has made me a millionaire. The thing about me is I don't forget where I come from, and I don't forget who was in my corner. When I had nothing, I knew I had Darius by my side. When I had everything, I had Darius by my side. All I wanted to do was pay the man back for always being there for me. Clearly, I couldn't, so I went to the next best thing," he explained.

"How did you find my address?" my mother side-eyed him.

He chuckled. "Sweetheart, I'm the law. I can find out anything. However, addresses are public records and Lemetti is not a common name. One thing I'll never do is forget about my brother." He leaned forward and turned a picture around and I gasped. It was a picture of him and my father. They had to be in their late teens. I couldn't stop the tears that welled in my eyes. I missed that damn man so much.

"So let me get this straight." My mother's eyes never left the picture. "You and my husband sold drugs together many, many years ago. He got out of the game, and you stayed in, but eventually went legit. He died, you continued on, and now you're handing over several million dollars to me and my kids as a thank you for him being by your side all those years ago?"

He nodded, "That's a way to sum it up."

"Wow."

"I know it's a lot to take in. I should have done this a lot sooner, but I toyed around with it for a while on how I could do it before I just said fuck it and did it."

The office became silent. I didn't know what to say.

"Look, I know it's a lot to take in. The money is there, ready to be distributed. It's all legit so it won't be flagged. I can write the checks from a legitimate, multi-million-dollar business, so they won't even look twice. If you want cold, hard cash, then we can do that too. My number is here on this business card. Feel free to take one and whenever you're ready, feel free to call or text me. It doesn't matter the day or time."

"Thank you, Mr. Jones," I finally spoke up. My mother stood up and I followed suit. "We will definitely be in touch." He nodded, as my mother, and I headed out. A lot had been dropped on us, starting with the fact that I was now a million dollars richer. I couldn't even wrap my head around it.

"Has your brother called you?" my mom asked as we made it to the parking lot. I pulled out my phone and didn't see any missed calls.

"No. I'll try him again." Placing the phone on speaker, I remote started my car.

"Yes, Deanna."

"Where are you? We were supposed to meet with the lawyer, remember?"

"It's been a damn day from hell and it's far from over. That shit completely slipped my mind. Everything good?"

"For the most part, yeah. But what happened?"

"Ain't shit for you to worry about."

"Well, it's something for me to worry about," my mama yelled. "What the hell happened?"

"My fuckin' house got raided. That's what the fuck happened," he snapped before he hung up. My eyes bucked and I looked at my phone, dialing his number back. He kept pushing my calls to voicemail, so I gave up.

"What the fuck is going on?" my mother groaned before she walked to her car, hopped in, and sped off. One thing she Monique Lemetti didn't play about was her kids, so I knew she was heading straight to my brother to get to the bottom of his shit.

Chapter Thirty - Four

Infinity Morrison

Today was crazy busy at the center. Between interviews, enrollments, and constant phone calls, I was beat, and it was only going on one in the afternoon. I left my watch at home and since I forgot to plug my phone in, it remained in my office on the charger. I finally got a moment to sit down after delivering lunches to all of the rooms. Snatching up my phone, my heart started racing when I saw a few missed calls from Ace and a text that said to not go to his house after I left work. I dialed his number but was met with voicemail. I tried a few more times and received the same response. I took a deep breath and shot him a text telling him that I was worried and to give me a call.

I closed my eyes and sat back. This was the stress my doctor was talking about that I didn't need. I placed my hand on my currently flat stomach and said I silent prayer for both my

277

unborn and my man. After a few moments, I sat back up to input attendance into the system and print out the invoices for weekly tuition. I smiled at the thought of three new staff members starting within the next week, which means I could also enroll more children. I couldn't lie, I was surprised at how well my center was taking off after being open for such a short amount of time. I thanked nobody but God and my son.

Before I knew it, it was pickup time. Thankfully, all of the parents had picked up their children by 4:45pm, so I was able to close a little early. Ace still hadn't called me back, so I tried to dial his number again. This time, it didn't even ring; the voicemail picked up immediately. I tried to pull up his location that we shared, but it showed no location found. I swallowed hard and tried not to worry. Instead, Gabby and I headed to Walmart to grab some things. Honestly, I don't think I needed anything, but I knew being home would just have me in constant fear and anxiety, so I figured being out the house would be best.

An hour and a half later, Gabby and I were leaving Walmart with a cart full of random shit. Just as I was loading the bags into the car, I felt my phone vibrating. Based on the ringtone playing through the AirPod, I knew it was Ace. I immediately tapped it to answer.

"Hey, where are you?" I shot off.

"Man, this has been a damn day from hell! Where y'all at?"

"Leaving Walmart."

"What the hell y'all get at Walmart?" he chuckled.

"A little bit of everything." I didn't miss him chuckle again. "Where are you?" I asked once more.

"My mama's. Come here. My location should be on."

"Okay."

We ended the call, and I finished putting the bags in. I strapped Gabby in and then pulled up Ace's location. Since traffic was light, I was at Ace's mother's house in no time. I saw his mother and his sister's cars parked in the driveway and his alongside the sidewalk. He must've been looking out the window because just as I put the car into park, he was walking down the walkway. I couldn't stop the smile that graced my face, and I didn't realize I was holding my breath until I let out a deep sigh. Laying my eyes on him and knowing he was okay, calmed me down.

"Hi," I spoke as he opened the back door to remove a sleeping Gabby.

"What's up, mama? Come on." I climbed out and made my way around the car to him. I immediately planted a kiss upon his lips.

"I'm glad you're okay," I admitted. He kissed my forehead and grabbed my hand as we walked towards his mother's front door.

"I'll always be good."

I didn't say anything as we headed inside. I saw his mother and sister both sitting on the couch, so I waved before sitting down on the opposite side next to Ace after he handed Gabby to his mother.

"Now that she's here, can you tell us what the fuck happened?" she wasted no time snapping. I looked over at Ace and he sighed before looking at the ground.

Ace began running down his day from the moment Gabby and I left the house this morning. I sat with my mouth agape as he spoke about how Los' house was raided, and then his house shortly after. He ended up contacting his lawyer to have the information pulled as to why their houses were raided and found out that one of his workers had ratted on him. I didn't miss the disappointment and hurt in his voice as he spoke.

"This is the shit I've been talkin' about, Deandre," his mother snapped. "I keep telling you this street shit is not forever! You have a fuckin' daughter now." In one motion she placed Gabby down, then stood up and was damn near in his face. "You wanna be a fuckin' thug forever but won't be happy until they pop yo ass or lock yo ass up and throw away the key. Your daughter is damn near eighteen fuckin' months and what have you done to get away from this shit? Huh?"

He sat there quietly for a moment but stared at his mother. I didn't miss the anger that flashed across his eyes.

"You swear you know what the fuck you're talkin' about, don't you?" he questioned. I couldn't lie, I was shocked because one thing Ace always took pride in was respecting his mother, but I could tell his shit was about to go left. "You swear a nigga has no goals, no ambition, no nothing except hustle, huh? When that shit is faithfully paying your mortgage and car note, you're not bitching. The moment when a little something happens, you want to preach like you're God."

"Deandre, please! I don't need your money to pay my bills. I've held that shit down since the day your father died. *YOU* decided you want to hustle. *YOU* decided to take over my payments. I never asked you for any of that shit. Did times get hard sometimes? Absolutely, but me being me, I always found a way to make shit work! What I'll never fuckin' do is allow you to throw some shit you decided to do up in my face like I asked you. Newsflash, Deandre, I don't need you to do shit for me! You need me more than I'll ever need you. Remember that shit."

At that moment, Ace tensed up. Looking in his eyes, I saw the anger dissipate and the hurt fill them. I tried to reach out and touch him, but he pulled away from me. His mother walked off with tears streaming down her face, and Ace looked as if he had just lost his best friend. Deanna sat stunned with her mouth hanging wide open. I looked at Ace again and his eyes remained staring in the direction his mother walked off toward. I tried again to touch him but was met with the same response. I nodded to myself before standing up and prepared myself to leave.

"You gonna leave a nigga too?" he questioned. "What, when shit gets tough, you're gonna fuckin' run?"

I twisted my face and looked at him like he lost his damn mind.

"I'm not even gonna answer that because I know you're in

your feelings due to the events that occurred today. When you're ready to talk to me like an adult, you know how to get in touch with me," I spoke evenly as I walked over, hugged his sister, and kissed Gabby.

He scoffed and then spoke again, "What, you gonna go through this pregnancy alone and then leave my child on the porch like Aaliyah did too?"

"DEANDRE!" his sister shrieked. Tears instantly pooled in my eyes as I looked at the first man who I gave my heart to since the loss of my son.

"Wow." I had finally found my voice, but it was shaky. I sniffled and wiped away the tear that fell. "Let me set the record straight. I'm nothing like that fuckin' girl. I would lay down and die before I ever leave my child on someone's fuckin' porch like they ain't shit to me. If I wanted to keep my child from you, I never would have fuckin' told you about my child. You got that though, Deandre. I promise you got that. From here on out, keep it strictly on a business transaction. You can bring Gabby to school and all that good shit, but you and I, I'm good on you. You clearly have some demons you still need to work through and before I stress myself out to the point where my unborn child's life is at risk again, I'll leave you alone."

With tears steadily streaming down my face, I walked out of his mother's house. My heart ached badly. If anybody knew how much I wanted another child, it would be Ace. On several occasions, I shared with him how the loss of my son affected me, so for him to think I would walk away from my child for a life that I didn't even live, was some shit that was killing me. I wasn't sure if this was some shit that Ace and I could bounce back from, but rather than stress over it, I was putting all of my focus and attention on having a healthy pregnancy. Bringing my child into this world was my only goal.

Chapter Thirty - Five

Deandre 'Ace' Lemetti

A week and a half later…

I fucked up, and I fucked up badly. I knew I fucked up, and honestly, I had no idea what the fuck to do. I hadn't even sent Gabby to daycare to avoid facing Infinity. I tried calling a few times, but she let my shit roll over to voicemail. My texts went unanswered. Even if I tried sending pictures of Gabby, she would simply react to the photo but say nothing.

I had hardly left my house over the last week. I ordered a shit ton of takeout, and Gabby watched damn near every fuckin' movie on Disney+ that was age appropriate. If anyone stopped by, I never bothered to answer. My phone remained charged, but I didn't answer anyone. I was sick. I missed my girl. I missed my mama. It felt weird as hell that even she wasn't speaking to me, but I knew she was in her feelings and as stubborn as she was,

285

she wouldn't make the first move to speak to me. I know it was hurting her even more not seeing Gabby.

I sighed as I pushed myself up from the couch. Gabby was sitting on the floor eating her goldfish snacks and watching Word Party. I scooped her up and headed toward our bedrooms. I grabbed a footed pajama out of her dresser since it was getting chilly. Once I had her changed, I threw on a pair of sweats over my ball shorts and snatched a hoodie up. I grabbed one of Gabby's fleece blankets, my keys, phone, and wallet and headed out the door.

As I drove, I didn't really have a destination in mind, but I knew I needed to get out of the house. Glancing down at the camera I had sitting on the dash that revealed the camera that pointed at Gabby, I noticed she had fallen asleep. Before I knew it, I found myself sitting in the parking lot at India Point Park. I was surprised at how empty it was. I put the car into park and sighed. Pulling out my phone, I opened my Instagram app and scrolled Infinity's profile. She hadn't posted much, but she did post a few random quotes on her story. Closing out of the app, I opened my messages to text her.

Me (7:27pm) – Hey mama. I hope you're feeling okay. Anything new on the baby? Is there anything you need from me?

I sent the message but remained on our thread with my fingers ready to type an additional message, but I didn't know exactly what to say. I waited a few minutes to see if she would respond, but just as it had been over the last few days, I got nothing.

Me (7:29pm) – Look, mama. I'm sorry. I was wrong as fuck for saying what I said. If it's one thing that I know for sure, it's that you are nothing like Aaliyah. I know what having this child means to you, so for me to be selfish at the time and say some shit like that was foul. Truthfully, I'm hurting without you, Ma. I miss the fuck out of you. I didn't realize how much I was used to you until you walked away from me...from us. I know Gabby misses you too. I get why you did it, and you had every right to do it too. I'll apologize until I'm blue in the face. Just come back to me. I need you.

I pushed send and then reread the message. I meant every word I said. I was lost without my girl. In such a short time, she had become a huge part of both mine and Gabby's lives and right now, neither of us were functioning properly without her; me more than Gabby. I stared at the phone for a few more minutes but still didn't even see so much as the bubbles jump to let me know she was typing. I sighed heavily. I put the car into gear and took off, heading off to continue to right my wrongs.

I pulled up to my mother's house fifteen minutes later. I killed the engine, grabbed Gabby, and headed to her front door. Her car was in the driveway, so I used my key to let myself in. She popped her head out from the kitchen just as I closed the door behind me.

"Hey," she spoke dryly.

"What's up?" I walked by her to go lay Gabby down in the

room my mother had here for her. Once she was in her bed, I grabbed the baby monitor and headed out of the room to talk to my mama. She was in the kitchen washing the few dishes she had, so I sat at the island behind her.

"I'm sorry, mama. I understand your fears and frustrations, trust me, I do. I was offended by you thinking I want nothing more than to be a hustler, when in reality, that is the furthest from the truth. Little do you know, the day this all happened, I was going to meet Los to let him know I was walking away. I finally got my legitimate business affairs in order and all the street shit was done. I just wanted to focus on my kids and my girl, that's it. But hearing you say that shit made me feel like that's all I would ever be to you."

"Deandre, I never wanted this life for you. Ever! You're better than the streets and could be anything you wanted. It may not make you rich as fast as the streets did, but it would have come with less risks. I hate this life for you. Has it afforded us an amazing lifestyle? Sure it has, but at what cost? You gotta watch your back everywhere you go. You can't move freely because you never know who is watching, scheming, or praying on your downfall. Add a baby into the mix and now she's at risk because they know the easiest way to get to you is through her. Hearing you say your house got raided was like all my fears coming true. This was the start of the downfall, and that's something I cannot handle."

My mother had tears streaming down her face. Here I had

been in the game damn near ten years and never had my mother shown this many emotions behind my decision. Yeah, she told me she was against it, but never had she sat me down and told me about her fears and shit behind it. I'm not sure if it would have influenced my decision to jump into it, but it would have remained in the back of my mind all these years.

"I already lost your father. I cannot fathom the idea of losing my son, my daughter, or my grandbaby. If I lost any of you, that's it for me. I cannot deal with another heartbreak like that."

"You don't have to worry about it, ma. That lifestyle is done. I handed over the reins, and my legit businesses have picked up and are doing well."

My mom nodded in approval. "Where's Infinity?"

I sighed heavily. I wasn't sure if Deanna had told my mother what had happened once she left the room, but I knew my mother was about to chew my ass out again.

"She ain't fuckin' with me," I admitted.

"What did you do?"

"I said some fucked up shit."

She sighed and shook her head.

"What did you say?" I replayed the conversation that I had with Infinity that same night. My mother's eyes became wide as saucers as she yanked the hand towel from her shoulder and snapped me with it. "I must've dropped you one too many got damn times for you to think that shit was okay."

"I never said it was okay. Trust me. I feel like shit. I haven't even brought Gabby to daycare so I could avoid her in hopes this shit blows over." I thought about mentioning the baby, but I remembered Infinity wanted to tell at her own time. Deanna hadn't even reached out to me about it, so I didn't know if she realized what Infinity was saying that night or not.

"You gotta fix that shit, Deandre."

"I've been trying but shit when I say she's not fuckin' with me, I mean it. She has all but blocked me. My calls and texts go unanswered. The most I get is a heart reaction on any picture I send her of Gabby. That's it. Not even gonna lie, Ma, I feel incomplete without her."

"That's your soulmate. I've always told you that you would know when you've met 'the one', and it looks like you've met her. Now it's up to you to fix your mistake and grow from here."

She smiled at me before I stood and went and gave her a hug.

"I love you."

"I love you more," she replied. "Leave my grandbaby here. The next time you keep her from me for this long, I'm filing for custody," she joked. I couldn't help but laugh because I knew she was going through Gabby withdrawals. After kissing my mother again, I headed out the door. This time, I was going to find my lady.

Chapter Thirty - Six
Infinity Morrison

I sighed as I walked through my front door and dropped my keys on the table.

"Don't jump," I heard Ace speak, but it was too late. I had jumped so hard I started pissing myself.

"What the fuck? What are you doing here?" I stood with my legs pressed closed. I couldn't believe this muthafucka just scared me enough to have me piss myself like I couldn't control my damn bladder. I rushed off to the bathroom, and I wasn't surprised that he followed me.

"We need to talk?"

"Why? You said what you said, so stand on it," I told him as I sat on the toilet.

"I didn't mean that shit, Infinity," he snapped.

"No, you did mean it. There are two types of people in this world that always tell the truth; that is a drunk person and an angry person. I don't know what the hell I ever did to you that would make you ever think I would do what Aaliyah did, but you feel that way. That's fine because I'm not going to fight and prove to you that I'm nothing like her. If my actions thus far haven't shown you that I'm different, then nothing ever will."

"Come on, man." He washed his hands over his face. He looked stressed and like he hadn't had a decent night's rest in days. "I love you, Infinity. I love you more than I've ever loved anyone else outside of my daughter. I know that you're nothing like Aaliyah. At the moment, I was hurting. I felt like my mama was turning her back on me, and then to see you get up and get ready to leave made me feel like you were doing it too, so I was saying shit to hurt you, and I was wrong as hell."

Here went these ridiculous ass tears that I was trying so hard to keep at bay. This was one thing I didn't miss about pregnancy. These emotions were a ghetto ass mess.

"How can I trust that every time you get mad, you won't try and compare me to her again? How do I know that when you're mad, you're not going to try and take my child from me?" I didn't miss the way his face twisted when I said that.

"I would never take our child from you."

"At this point, I no longer know what to believe. I also believed you wouldn't lash out at me and try and make me out to be a shitty ass mom-to-be, but you did," I reminded him. He rolled his eyes and sighed heavily.

"What do I have to do to show you that I'm truly sorry?" I

searched his eyes, and I could see the regret in them. I could see the sincerity in them. But I also saw the stress, and with me wanting a healthy and stress-free pregnancy, I didn't know if trying to help him with his stress was a smart idea.

"Give me time. My feelings are truly hurt, Deandre. You of all people know what my son means to me. You of all people knew about my dreams of wanting to become a mom. There isn't much you don't know about me, especially when it comes to this journey of wanting to be a parent. Yet, when you were angry, none of that mattered. You didn't care about my feelings, and that is something that I am struggling to deal with. I love you, Deandre. I love you more than you'll ever know, but this time, I have to put me first. I have to put my unborn child first."

The space between us became quiet. The tears were falling from my eyes faster than I could even wipe them away. This was literally one of the hardest things I've had to do because I enjoyed Deandre. I enjoyed everything about him, so for me to force myself away from him was lowkey killing me.

"We're not breaking up, Infinity," he stated sternly. Instead of responding, I shrugged. At this point, whatever we had was being put on the back burner. I needed to focus on my business and my baby; nothing else mattered. I was still leaning against the sink when Ace came over and planted a kiss on my temple. I closed my eyes to enjoy the moment. "Keep me updated on everything regarding you and my baby. I'm not playing. No detail is too small. I don't care if you have a craving at 4am, I better be the one you call." I laughed because I knew he was dead ass serious. He missed all of this during Aaliyah's pregnancy with Gabby, so he was trying to take advantage and be there for everything. He kissed my temple again before he walked out. I heard the front door close, and it was at that moment where I broke down. I slid down the sink and onto the floor of the bathroom. I was starting to question why God seemed to keep putting me in these fucked up love situations. I just wanted to love the right man and wanted him to love me back with no bullshit attached. Now here I was pregnant again, by a man who was already a great father but seemed to have some doubt that I wouldn't pull the same shit his baby's mother pulled.

After letting out my final cry, I picked myself up and turned on the shower. I truly didn't know where Ace and I were heading from here. During the shower, I closed my eyes and asked God to guide me through this difficult time and if it was meant to be, bring Ace and I back together stronger than ever.

*****

Five Months Later...

I waddled through the center and tried to catch my breath at the same time. I felt like a damn whale, and this little girl giving me all types of pelvic pain wasn't making it any better. I was now thirty-five weeks pregnant and truthfully, I was miserable. Dr. Denson agreed to pull me out of work at thirty-six weeks so that I would be on bed rest for the remainder of my pregnancy. So far, everything has gone smoothly, except I ate everything under the sun and have gained almost thirty pounds.

I just finished delivering the last lunch cart to the toddler room and was sitting behind the front desk. I kicked my shoes off under the desk and stretched my toes while rotating my ankle. I closed my eyes and took a few deep breaths. As much as I loved working for myself, I was looking forward to being taken out of work. I was done. They could stick a fork in me.

My phone vibrated on the desk, capturing my attention. Looking down, I saw it was the camera for the center. Glancing at the door, I saw Ace standing there. I smiled as I used my phone to unlock the door. It had been months since the incident at his mother's happened, and I still kept my guard up, but I would be lying if I said he wasn't working his ass off to prove he truly was apologetic. I was hesitant to fully give in, but he was definitely breaking down the wall I had built up.

"Hey," I greeted as he made his way to the counter.

"What's going on? How are you feeling?"

"Large and tired. I'm pretty sure my feet are going to be swollen again. I can't wait for this week to be over," I admitted.

"Almost there, mama. Did you eat today?"

"I eat like a million times a day. You know I keep my snacks stashed in my desk," I chuckled. I wasn't lying though. I probably had more snacks than office supplies in my desk at the moment.

"Do you want food?" he asked.

"What do you have in mind?"

"Whatever your heart desires." I paused for a moment and thought about it.

"Hawaiian pizza," I told him.

"Pineapples don't go on pizza, ma."

"Oh yes it does. Your daughter says so."

We both laughed. It didn't matter how much he judged my cravings; he always got them without so much as a complaint.

"A'ight. Order it and I'll go pick it up. Did Aaliyah bring Gabby to school today?"

I sat up in the chair to check the computer system. Over the last few months, Ace and Aaliyah's custody agreement changed. She went from supervised visits, to unsupervised visits, to now she got to keep Gabby overnight every other weekend and one day during the week. The day of the week varied based on her and Ace's schedule, but it worked for them.

"Yeah, she's here." He didn't respond verbally, but I did catch the nod. I pulled out my phone and ordered myself a medium pizza and Ace a medium pizza. "After work, can you go with me to Walmart?"

"What the hell do you need from Walmart now, woman? You don' bought everything they have for baby's and specifically for girls."

"Oh, shut up. I need breast pads."

"What the fuck is a breast pad?"

"They go in my bra so that if I leak, rather than wetting the bra, it'll soak up in the pad." He shook his head.

"The shit they come up with. Is that all you need?"

"Yeah, I think so."

Although this is the furthest that I've made it in pregnancy, and so far, everything was going smoothly, I opted out of having a baby shower. I didn't want to be the center of attention, and I didn't have many people that I would invite anyway, so Ace and I just bought everything our daughter would need. He set up a nursery at both his place and mine. Ace had been trying to convince me to give up my townhouse, but I refused. I needed to have a place to escape when he pissed me off. We were back to alternating where we spent time whether it was my place or his, but it worked for us. I had a bag packed at both houses in case I went into labor. Each of us had our own car seat bases for our cars, and I kept the baby stroller at my place.

Ace and I made small talk before he left to go get the food. I sat back in the chair and rubbed my stomach as I felt my baby girl move. We still hadn't decided on a name for her yet, but I was sure once I saw her, it would come to me with no problem.

The bottom of my stomach cramped a little, so I rubbed that area, and within about thirty seconds, it had gone away. I had been having contractions on and off for a few weeks, but I was only dilated to one centimeter. Dr. Denson had advised me that if the baby did decide to come a little earlier, she wasn't going to stop labor. I prayed she stayed put for a few more weeks, but it ultimately was up to her. I was ready for her either way.

Twenty minutes later, Ace returned with the food. We went into my office where we both ate, and he pitched off a few baby names that I wasn't a fan of. He was trying to stick with the 'G' thing to go with Gabby, but nothing stood out to me.

"Can you bring Gabby home with you?" he asked.

"If I can make it through the day. I've been having these stupid contractions on and off all day."

"Do we need to call Dr. Denson?"

"Nah, they aren't strong or consistent. They're just annoying."

He side-eyed me before he spoke again.

"A'ight man. I'll be here to pick her up. If you need me, call me."

"I will," I assured him. He planted a kiss on my lips followed by my forehead before he headed out of the building. I told him that I was okay, but honestly, something was telling me that this little girl would be making her appearance sooner rather than later.

Chapter Thirty - Seven

Deandre 'Ace' Lemetti

These last few months had been crazy. It's been a bigger adjustment than I could have ever imagined. I was officially done with the streets minus one loose end that was getting tied up tonight. I had to let the heat die down before I could react, but I know the nigga thought I forgot. It was nothing for my lawyer to get her hands on who initiated the raid. That bitch nigga Sly was pissed that his ass got popped. Rather than take that shit like a man on the chin, he decided to go singing to the boys in blue. Los switched up the whole operation and even moved from his crib. His ass was tired of looking over his shoulder. I didn't blame him. The only reason I hadn't moved is because I wanted my next spot to be one that Infinity and I copped together, but her ass was stalling on the living together shit for whatever reason.

Anyway, it took some time and serious dough, but someone

down at the station that my lawyer knew personally, was able to get me a copy of the shit this nigga was singing about. The shit he told them, there was no wonder why the cops showed up the way they did. This nigga made them think we were Griselda Blanco or some shit. He told them we had rooms with keys from floor to ceiling, and wads and wads of cash. His dumb ass didn't realize that he had a better chance of giving them the location to the warehouse for them to find shit. It was what it was though, and shit was moved. Los revamped the entire operation and even kept Sly's ass on to keep him close. He didn't work directly with him, and Los had eyes on him at all times. The nigga would have no idea what would hit him.

In the meantime though, I was on the countdown until my daughter arrived. Shit had been smooth for the most part between Infinity and me. I could tell she was still a little skeptical, but she had let her guard down. I truly felt fucked up about the shit I said, and I meant every word when I said I would do whatever I have to in order to make it up to her and I had been doing just that.

My phone rang just as I was pulling up to a redlight. I raised an eyebrow when I saw that it was Aaliyah.

"Yo," I answered.

"Hey, sorry to bother you. I know it's not typically my day, but I was wondering if I could pick Gabby up from daycare and keep her for a few hours," she questioned.

"Is everything good?" I purposely bypassed her question.

"Yeah. My mom just told me that my grandparents came into town as a surprise, and I wanted Gabby to meet them. I will bring her back tonight, just let me know what time works best for you."

"A'ight. I'll let Infinity know you're picking her up."

"Let her know?" she inquired.

"Yes, so she can let the staff know. They know you typically only pick her up once a week, so the fact that this would be the second time, I don't want any issues."

She sighed, and I was waiting for her to pop off, but instead she said okay and thanked me before ending the call.

I had to admit; Aaliyah had been doing the damn thing with this mother thing. I was concerned about having her around my child initially due to the circumstances, but one thing was evident now; she loved Gabby and Gabby loved her too.

As I continued on my drive, I FaceTime'd Los.

"Why the fuck you hitting me on FaceTime? I ain't your bitch, nigga," he joked.

"First of all, chill with the bitch shit. Second of all, don't act dumb." He knew just like I knew that FaceTime calls couldn't ever be tapped, so it was how I spoke to anyone whenever I needed to make a call that could incriminate me. "Shit's all good?"

"Yeah. Tonight it's done."

I nodded, "Cool. Cool. A'ight, I just wanted to make sure."

"You know I'm on top of shit. Just make sure you on the

money, nigga. No fuck ups."

"Never that."

"Bet. I'll holla."

"Fa'sho."

We ended the call and I pulled into Walmart. I figured since I had some time to kill, I would get these damn nipple pads that Infinity had mentioned. The last thing I wanted her to do was walk around being uncomfortable, and I damn sure didn't want to be dragged through Walmart later while she melted over baby clothes. One thing was for sure, my daughter needed absolutely nothing. Infinity was on top of every damn thing. My mother and sister wanted to throw her a baby shower, but she was adamant about not having one. She even said if they tried to throw a surprise one, she would walk right out. The crazy part is, I believed her. My mother indeed planned on throwing her a surprise shower, but I told her to respect her wishes of not doing it. My mother and Deanna were excited for the new baby to come. This was different for all of us. Infinity kept my mother and sister included with everything regarding the pregnancy and updated them after each appointment. We were robbed of this with Gabby, so we were all cherishing it.

I walked into Walmart and headed right for the baby section. Thankfully, I was able to find what I was looking for rather quickly. I grabbed the biggest box that I could find and headed straight back toward the register. I placed the box on the belt and reached into my pocket to grab my wallet. I didn't miss shorty giving me the eye, but I wasn't about to entertain her.

"You're handsome," she told me, rather than giving me the total. Looking at the screen, I peeled off a ten-dollar bill and placed it on the counter.

"Thank you, I'm also married. Keep the change and buy a water, ma. Thirst isn't a good look for you." I winked, grabbed the bag, and walked off. Some females were bold as hell when it came to tryna talk to a dude. They would literally see you with your woman and shoot their shot. I shook my head at the thought. I sent Infinity a text letting her know that I had gotten what she needed from Walmart and that Aaliyah was grabbing Gabby, so she could go home after work and relax. I didn't know how much time we had left before baby girl graced us with her presence, but I was ready.

*****

Later That Night...

"You good, mama?" I asked Infinity as she climbed into the bed. She looked a little uncomfortable, but she was tolerating.

"Yeah. Where you going?"

"I gotta run out and meet Los real quick, and then I'll be back." She looked at me with a side eye and I knew she wanted to ask more questions, but she didn't. "I won't be long, I promise. If you need me, call me." She nodded and climbed under the blanket. I kissed her forehead and pulled the blanket up to her neck. I knew it wouldn't be long before she was knocked out. On the way out, I stopped in Gabby's room and peeked on her. She was sound asleep.

Within twenty-five minutes, I pulled up to Los' new spot. I pulled my car into his garage, and he immediately closed it behind me. I went through the garage door and into his house. He was standing by his back door waiting for me.

"What's good, nigga? You ready?" Reaching into the kitchen drawer, I grabbed the black leather gloves and the piece I knew he would have waiting for me.

"Always," he responded. I pulled out my phone, silenced it and left it on the counter at Los'. I prayed that Infinity wouldn't call me while I was gone, but I absolutely couldn't take the phone with me. We headed out the backdoor and walked across his dark yard.

"You ain't got shit that's about to pop out on a nigga, do you?" I asked, half joking.

"Nah nigga, ain't shit back here. We do gotta hop the fence though."

"What the fuck? Nigga, I ain't hopped a damn fence in years."

"Well figure out how you're gonna do it and shut up." I sucked my teeth and shook my head as Los hopped over the fence. I hiked my sweats up and was sure to keep the piece in place. Just as I did when I was a teen, I hopped the fence easily. We landed in the yard of an abandoned spot that had a dark colored beater in the driveway.

"How you find this spot?"

He side-eyed me as if I asked a stupid question.

"It's behind my house. How else do you think I found it, nigga?" I chuckled because he had me there. We climbed in and he started it up. I had to admit, it looked like a piece of shit but ran quiet as shit. We didn't speak as Los headed to the spot where he knew Sly was.

"So what's the plan?"

"Shit, he's at a trap. The nigga who he's side by side with knows the deal, so he's just gonna walk away. He's gonna help them clean up once it's all said and done. Business won't be affected at all," he explained.

"You're sure this will work?"

"As long as my name is Los."

"Well actually, nigga, it's Dion," I reminded him. We both burst into laughter as he flipped me off. Los hated his name, so he went by Los, which was short for his middle name Carlos. He had gone by Los for as long as I could remember, and if anyone tried calling him Dion outside of his mama, he was stealing off in their shit.

Ten minutes later, we pulled onto the street. I was surprised it was as dead as it was, but that was good for us. He let the car run idle as we climbed out. I adjusted the gun on my waist and followed Los. I was expecting him to go through a side or back door, but this nigga went straight up to the porch.

"Here," he said pulling something out of his pocket. I noticed it was a silencer, so I removed my piece and quickly screwed it on as he let himself into the spot. Just like he said, Sly was there alone. The only difference was he was knocked the fuck out on the couch. I scoffed and shook my head.

"Wake up, bitch," I gritted, knocking him upside the head with the butt of the gun, but not hard enough to knock his ass out cold.

"What the fuck?" He sat up rubbing his head. I didn't even bother to hide my face because after this, he would never see my face again.

"You thought you would be able to have my shit raided and I let that shit go?" I could see the fear in his eye, and it was comical. "When you stole from me, I let that shit go. I told you just work it off, but no. Your dumb ass had to go singing like a fuckin' canary. Why the fuck would you continue to bite the hand that feeds you? Ain't no way you could be that dumb," I ranted. He looked as if he wanted to say so much, but he had nothing to say. I didn't miss the tear that rolled down his cheek. "Give me one good reason why I shouldn't pop yo ass right now?"

This time, he looked up at me and smirked.

"If I make it out of here, I'm killin' yo ass and fuckin' yo bitch." I immediately brought the gun back and came down across his face. His head snapped to the side and his mouth instantly began bleeding.

"Nigga, you couldn't even fuck my bitch in your dreams." I

came down across his face again. I wasn't even about tire myself out by beating his ass. I came here for one thing, and one thing only, and that was to pop this nigga.

Just as I cocked the gun back, his head exploded like a watermelon. I instantly looked at Los.

"I wasn't about to let you have that shit on your conscious. You got out of these streets for a reason. I just wanted you to release some anger on his ass first."

I grinned and dapped him up. He pulled out his burner phone, sent a text, and we walked out the same way we came in. The ride back to his crib was silent as I thought about what had just happened. It was finally over. It was time to focus on my businesses, my girl, and my kids.

When we arrived back to Los', I gave him the gloves and gun before dapping him up again. Just as I scooped up my phone, I saw a text from Infinity.

Wifey (11:21pm) – *It's time!*

My heart immediately started racing. I rushed out of the house, jumped into my car, and peeled off. I was thankful that Los had opened his garage. I knew I was breaking every single traffic violation known, but right now, I didn't give a shit.

I dialed Deanna but didn't get an answer. I dialed my mother but was met with the same response. I sighed. I tried both my mother and Deanna again but received the same results. Frustrated, I scrolled until I came across Aaliyah's name. Tapping her name, I placed the phone to my ear.

"Hey, is everything okay?" she answered.

"Yeah, everything is cool. Sorry to wake you up. I need you to meet me at my house," I told her.

"Okay. Is Gabby okay?"

"Gabby is fine," I chuckled. "My girl is in labor, and I can't get in touch with my mama or sister to pick her up."

"Oh shit. Okay, I'll be right there." I could hear her shuffling, so I knew she was rushing.

"I appreciate it for real."

We ended the call just as I pulled up to the house. I could see the bedroom light on and could see Infinity pacing back and forth.

It was showtime!

Epilogue

Infinity Morrison

I did not remember these contractions feeling like this! I felt as if I was about to shit myself every time a contraction hit. They had been coming every seven to ten minutes, but they were hard to breathe through. Ace had just taken Gabby outside to put her into her mother's car. I was looking around the room to make sure I had everything because I was sure that I was being kept.

I headed down the stairs just as Ace was closing the door behind him. He grabbed my hospital bag and the baby's hospital bag that we kept by the door.

"You ready?" he asked. I simply nodded as I waddled outside. He tossed our bags in the back and helped me get into the car. I couldn't lie, I was a little nervous seeing as how I hadn't even made it to thirty-six weeks. Ace sped out of the driveway and headed toward the hospital.

"Can you slow down? I would like to make it in one piece."
Before he could respond, I felt a gush of fluid between my legs.
"Oh shit."

"What?"

"My water broke."

"In my car?!" Ace hollered.

"Uhhh, I think so," I answered sarcastically. I could see his jaw flex, but he would be okay. It wasn't like I pissed myself all over his car. I could feel another contraction hitting and braced myself for it. Thankfully, it passed and once it did, I shot my mother a text letting her know that I was in labor and would have Ace keep her updated.

We made it to the hospital in less than fifteen minutes and thankfully, there was a parking spot right in the front. Once Ace parked, he came around and helped me out. We went into the triage area where I checked in and was instantly taken back for my vitals to be checked. It seemed as if my daughter wanted to show her ass because I swore that I had three or four contractions in the five damn minutes it took them to check my vitals.

Ace and I were guided into a smaller exam room where we waited for the doctor to come in. I changed into one of those gowns that had everything out. I couldn't wait to give birth and put on one of my damn Walmart nightgowns.

Ten minutes later, the doctor came in and introduced himself. He let me know that he was going to check my cervix for dilation and explained it would be uncomfortable. He wasn't lying either. That shit felt weird as hell. I swear I didn't remember any of this with my son. Either it just happened *that* fast, or I was so disconnected from the outside world that I didn't pay attention.

"Alright, you're about five centimeters and fifty percent effaced."

"What does that mean?" Ace asked.

"It means we'll be having a baby within the next twelve to twenty-four hours. I'll go ahead and page Dr. Denson. Is there anything I can do for you?" I shook my head. "Alright, transport will be here shortly to get you up to labor and delivery."

I took a few deep breaths because the nerves were kicking in. It was happening. I was giving birth to an almost full-term baby, and I couldn't wait.

*****

Five Hours Later...

"That's it, Infinity," Dr. Denson cheered me on. I was fuckin' exhausted. I had been pushing for just under an hour and I felt like I wasn't doing shit. Ace assured me that I was doing great, but I felt like I was just trying to shit without the urge. "Alright. She is right there, so I need one good, strong push from you."

I took a few deep breaths as Ace ran a cold rag across my head. He planted a kiss on my forehead and told me how well I was doing. At the moment, I wanted him to shut the fuck up because I was tired of pushing.

I propped myself up on my elbows as I felt a contraction starting, and I began pushing. This time I felt like I was doing something and clearly, I was because Dr. Denson's voice became super excited.

"I can see her head, Infinity. One more good push and she's here, I promise." She better had meant this shit because I was two seconds from telling them to leave her ass right inside. I took a few more deep breaths before pushing again. This time they told me to slow down because her head came out and they had to suction her. I was starting to panic because I could hear them suctioning her mouth and talking to her, but she wasn't crying.

"Alright, one small push to get the shoulders and we're good. One, two, three..."

I pushed with all my might and felt her slide out and before I knew it, the room filled with the most beautiful sound I had ever heard. I instantly burst into tears. She was here. My baby girl was here. I did it. I was a mother.

They placed her on my chest, and I instantly fell in love with her. She was everything I hoped she would be. Even for being over four weeks early, she had a helluva set of lungs on her, and if I had to guess, she was a good seven pounds.

Dr. Denson explained to me how to deliver the placenta, and that she had to insert a small stitch from where the baby ripped me.

Once the room calmed down, I laid there staring at my

daughter. Ace remained by my side looking at the creation we created that was ever so beautiful.

"Giselle," I spoke. "Giselle Mercedes Lemetti." Ace smiled because he pitched the name Giselle to me a few times, and I kept telling him I wasn't sold on it, but she looked like Giselle would fit her.

"Only if you do the honor of joining the Lemetti Legacy," Ace said as he pulled something out of his pocket. My mouth dropped and when he flipped the lid, I started crying. The ring was beautiful. I had spoken a million times about how much I loved halo-setting rings, and he made sure this ring was a halo-setting. "Will you marry me, Infinity?"

I couldn't even say anything. Instead, I just nodded. He slipped the ring on my finger and the room erupted into applause. I didn't even notice the doctors and nurses returning to check on us. I was so wrapped up in my daughter.

My daughter. I actually had my own baby. After years of working with children and losing my son, I was blessed with the most perfect little girl ever. I closed my eyes and thanked my son because I knew he was behind me getting another chance in the form of a little girl.

I had no idea where this journey between Ace and I was heading, but with our babies buckled up in the back, I was ready to ride front and center alongside him.

"Thank you, ma," Ace said.

"For what?"

"For being you. Before Gabby, I knew nothing about love beyond my mother and sister. Gabby came in and changed that shit instantly. From day one, you took care of my baby girl. They always say the quickest way to a niggas heart is through his stomach, but truthfully, it's through his children. Watching you not only love my daughter the way you do, but also birth another daughter of mine, I owe you for life. Simply put, thank you for holding onto the key to a hustla's heart and allowing me to believe in love again. I love you forever."

"I love you more."

I guess we could say our family was complete. At least for now anyway.

The End!

About The Author

Leondra LeRae grew up in Providence, RI. She is the mother of two, and her children are her pride and joy. She has dreams of becoming a mental health therapist but enjoys writing in her free time. At 19, she self-published her first urban fiction novel

At 20 years old, Leondra signed with SBR Publications where she released National Best Seller; Official Street Queen. To date, Leondra LeRae has published more than twenty novels which all can be found on Amazon.

Feel free to interact with her
Like her fan page:
www.facebook.com/AuthorLeondraLeRae
Follow her on Twitter: www.twitter.com/LeondraLeRae
Instagram: www.instagram.com/leondralerae
Email: authorleondralerae@gmail.com

Select Any Other of Her Reads on Amazon at:
www.amazon.com/author/leondralerae

Made in the USA
Middletown, DE
31 October 2023